Strange Case of Dr. Jekyll and Mr. Hyde

化身博士

中英對照雙語版

Robert Louis Stevenson

羅伯特・路易斯・史蒂文森 —— 著

陳家瑩 —— 譯

笛藤出版

我大膽地推測，最終人們會理解

人都是擁有多種樣貌、矛盾卻又獨立的群體。

Strange Case of
Dr. Jekyll
and
Mr. Hyde

化身博士

目錄

contents

Chapter

門的故事

01

你丟出一個問題，就像推動一顆石頭。
你安靜地坐在山丘上，然後石頭往下滾去，
連帶地其他的石頭也滾動下山。

　　律師厄特森先生外表粗曠，身材瘦長，給人一種冷淡疏離又不苟言笑的感覺，但大家還是很喜歡他。在氣氛融洽的聚會中，只要一喝到美味的葡萄酒，他的雙眼就會散發出溫暖的光芒。這種情懷平日只會從他的行為舉止中展現，只有在飽餐一頓後，也才有機會從他的言談中聽出這種幽微情懷。他律己甚嚴，獨處時只喝琴酒以克制自己對美酒的渴望，雖然熱愛戲劇，但已經二十年沒踏足劇院。相反地，他卻以非常寬厚的態度對待他人，有時會懷著近乎欽羨的心情，看待他人因為犯錯而承受的高度精神壓力，同時極力提供協助，而非責備。他常古怪地說：「我傾向採取該隱[1]的做法，不干涉他人的生活，讓我的兄弟選擇惡魔的道路。」因此，對走上歧途的人，他經常成為那些人此生中最後一位有名望又善良的朋友。在這樣的前提之下，只要他們來到他的辦公室，他就絕不會另眼相待。

　　毫無疑問，這對厄特森先生來說完全不成問題，因為他天性含蓄，友誼也是建立在這樣寬宏良善的基礎之上。性格謙遜的人交友隨緣，這位律師也是如此。他的朋友不是和他有血緣關係，就是相識很久的知交，和常春藤無異，他的情感是隨著時間慢慢積累，和對象是否合適則全然無關。

　　他和遠房表親，也是城內眾所周知的理查恩菲爾先生，就維持著這樣的關係。對很多人來說，他們倆究竟從對方身上看到什麼，或有什麼共通話題，實在令人不解。他們會在週日時

1　該隱與亞伯是亞當和夏娃所生下的兩個兒子。該隱是農民，他的弟弟亞伯為一個牧羊人。該隱是神話史上第一個謀殺他人的人類，亞伯是第一個死去的人類。

一起散步，根據看到的人說，他們之間的氣氛沉悶，一言不發，遇到朋友時則會像鬆了一口氣般地打招呼。即便如此，這場散步對他們來說仍是每週最重要的事。他們不僅會為此放棄平日的娛樂，甚至還會推辭跟工作相關的應酬。如此一來，才能在全然不受干擾的狀態下享受這場散步。

　　他們倆在某次散步時，走入一條位於倫敦繁忙街區中的巷弄。巷道雖小又安靜，但在週間生意十分繁忙。居民們似乎都很會做生意，也希望生意能變得更好，還會把剩下的穀物都展示出來，炫耀意味十足。街道裡的店面就像是一排排微笑的售貨小姐，笑容可掬地邀請大家入內。就算在週日，街道沒有了日常的艷麗樣貌，人潮也不如平常的熙來攘往，這條街道和四周黯淡的街區相比，仍舊耀眼如森林裡的野火。新油漆好的百葉窗，晶亮的黃銅器具還有乾淨又歡樂的氛圍，讓路過的行人眼前為之一亮。

　　往東方的左手邊走去，過了某轉角的兩扇門之後，整齊劃一的街道線條被一個庭園的入口切斷。那裡有一棟外觀陰森的房子。它的外牆向外延伸到了街道之上，那是棟兩層樓的建築物，沒有窗戶，一樓只有一扇門，樓上則是一面無色的外牆。誰都看得出來整棟房子已荒廢多時，乏人看管了。門板不但起泡又褪色，上面沒有門鈴也沒有門環。流浪漢無精打采地走向壁龕，在鑲板上點燃火柴，小朋友在臺階上擺攤開店，學生則拿著小刀在裝飾邊條上亂劃。近十年的時間裡，沒有任何人出現趕走這些人，或是修補它被破壞的地方。

　　恩菲爾先生和律師走在那條街對面，當他們靠近入口時，

恩菲爾舉起了手杖指著它說,

「你注意過那扇門嗎?」等他的同伴肯定的回應後,他接著說「我認為它和一件奇怪的事有關。」

「是嗎?是什麼事呢?」厄特曼先生的語調微微地變了。

恩菲爾先生回答說:「事情是這樣的。那晚約凌晨三點,是個漆黑的冬夜,我正從遙遠的地方趕路回家。在回家的路上我經過一個小鎮,那裡除了路燈,什麼都沒有。一條條的街道,所有人都沉沉睡著。每條街都像是要舉辦遊行一樣燈火通明,但卻又空空蕩蕩,就像教堂一樣。到最後我有點害怕,開始留意附近環境,仔細聽著四周的聲響,希望能看到一個警察。突然間,我看到兩個人,一位是身材矮小的男人,朝著東方快步前進,另一個則是一個小女孩,大約八到十歲的年紀,她拚命地快跑過街。那兩個人在轉角處相撞,然後可怕的事就發生了。那個男人竟然毫不在乎地踩過那個小女孩的身體,就讓她躺在地上尖叫。雖然現在聽起來好像沒什麼,但是當下的情景非常可怕。那不像是一個人,反而像台要命的重型貨車。我大叫出聲,拔腿追上那個男人,把他抓回現場,那時已經有不少人在現場圍觀。

他非常冷靜完全沒有反抗的意思,但用極為惡毒的眼神瞪著我,讓我留了一身冷汗,就像剛跑完步一樣。那些出現的人都是小女孩的家人,很快地,她的醫生也來了。醫生說女孩沒有什麼大礙,只是受到驚嚇,你可能認為事情就這樣結束了吧。但奇怪的事發生了，我看那個男人的第一眼就討厭他，那女孩的家人也是如此，這是非常自然的事。但那位醫生的態度卻讓我難以忘懷。他是一位平凡普通的藥劑師，年齡或膚色都非常一般，有著濃厚的愛丁堡口音，情緒卻像風笛一樣激動。他和我們一樣，只要一看到那個男人就氣得臉色發白，恨不得把他殺了。我們彼此都知道心裡在想什麼，既然殺人是不可能的事，我們就選擇了第二種比較可行的方法。

我們告訴那個男人，我們絕對會讓這個醜聞在倫敦傳開，徹底毀了他的名譽，就算他有朋友或享有盛名，我們也會搞得他身敗名裂。我們一邊激動跟他理論，一邊阻止那些想要找他算帳的女人們，她們全都氣瘋了。我沒見過那麼多憤恨難平的人，但那個男人卻像置身事外一樣，態度冷酷又輕蔑，雖然我看得出來他也害怕，但他卻能像惡魔一樣應付這一切。

「如果你們要利用這件事情得到金錢，我當然沒辦法說不。每位紳士都希望能避免爭執。開個價錢吧。」他說。我們幫那女孩的家人要了一百英鎊，他當然不想同意，但我們這些人是很麻煩的，到最後他就妥協了。接下來就是去拿錢，你猜他帶我們去哪了？就是那個有門的房子！他拿出鑰匙開門，進去拿了十英磅的金幣和一張顧資銀行的支票，上面寫了持票人可以簽領的金額，還簽了一個我不能透露的名字，雖然那個名字是整個故事的重點之一。他是一個非常有名望的人，而且時常見報。支票上的金額是死的，但如果他的簽名是真的，這張支票會變得更值錢。

我自作主張地跟那個人說，這整件事非常可疑。在現實生活裡，不會有人可以在凌晨四點走進一扇地窖的門，然後拿出一張將近一百英鎊的支票，上頭還簽著別人的名字。但他態度隨意又輕蔑地回答我「別擔心，我會跟著你們等到銀行開門，再親自去兌現這張支票。」於是，我們所有人一起出發，包括那位醫生，女孩的爸爸，那個男人和我自己，全都到我的辦公室度過下半夜。等到隔天，等我們吃完早餐後，大家一起去了銀行。我親自把那張支票交給銀行櫃檯，告訴他們我覺得這是一張偽造的票券。但事實並非如此，那張支票是真的。

「嘖嘖！」厄特曼先生嘆了口氣

「看來我們的想法一致，」恩菲爾先生說。「沒錯，這是個很糟糕的故事。那男人是個讓人難以忍受的傢伙，該死的大壞蛋。但開支票的確是一位德高望重的仕紳，還是位人人稱善的大好人（這點最糟糕）。我猜一定和敲詐勒索有關。那位正直的人因為年輕時犯下的一些荒唐事，所以付出這樣高昂的代價。也因為這樣，我把那棟房子稱為「勒索之屋」。但就算這樣推論，也遠遠無法解釋發生的一切。」他接著說，然後陷入沉思之中。

厄特森先生突然提問，把他飄遠的思緒拉回，「你無法確定開支票的人是否住在那棟房子裡，對吧？」

「可能性很高，不是嗎？」恩菲爾先生回答。「但我恰巧看到他的地址，他住在某個廣場裡。」

「你也從沒問過那棟房子的情況嗎？」厄特森先生說。

「不，先生。我行事小心。」是他的回答。「我對發問非常小心，因為一不注意就會變得像在法庭審判那樣。你丟出一個問題，就像推動一顆石頭。你安靜地坐在山丘上，然後石頭往下滾去，連帶地其他的石頭也滾動下山。接著，在最料想不到的時候，石頭就打中某個在後花園的溫和老傢伙，接著整個家族就得改名換姓。不，先生，我有自己的原則，看來越奇怪的事，我就越不發問。」

「這是個非常好的原則。」那位律師說

「但我自己也查看過那個地方，」恩菲爾先生繼續說。「那幾乎不能算是一棟房子。它只有一扇門，除了我這次遇到的那位先生外，沒有別人進出過那扇門。二樓有三個面朝庭院的窗戶，一樓則完全沒有窗戶。而窗戶雖然總是關著，但保持地相當乾淨整潔。房子的煙囪通常都冒著煙，所以一定有人住在那。但我也不是很確定，因為附近的房子很密集，實在很難分辨得出每一戶的區隔。」

這倆個人再度沉默地走了一會兒，接著厄特森先生說，「恩菲爾，你的那個原則很不錯。」

「我也這麼認為」恩菲爾回答。

「話雖如此，」那位律師繼續說，「我想知道那個撞倒小女孩，又踩過她身體的男人叫什麼名字。」

　　「好吧，」恩菲爾先生說，「我不認為讓你知道會有什麼壞處。他的名字叫做海德。」

　　「嗯，」厄特森先生說，「他是個什麼樣的人？」

　　「他的樣子很難形容。外表看上去有點不對勁，給人一種強烈的違和感。我從沒見過這麼不討喜的人，但原因我也說不上來。我有種強烈的感覺，他身體一定有畸形的地方，但我沒辦法確切指出位置。不，先生，我沒辦法形容他的樣子，這絕不是因為我記憶力不好，因為我現在都能清楚地看到他的臉。」

　　厄特森先生再度陷入沉默，邊走邊沉思。「你確定他用了鑰匙？」他最後問道。「親愛的先生…」恩菲爾先生驚訝地不知道該怎麼回答才好。厄特森先生接著說，「是的，我知道這一切都很奇怪。事實上，我沒有問你另一方的名字，是因為我已經知道了。理查，這故事你告訴我是正確的選擇。如果剛剛的細節有任何不正確的地方，最好修改一下。」

　　「你一開始就可以提醒我的，」恩菲爾先生帶著一絲不悅回答，「但我說的全是事實。那個傢伙有一把鑰匙，而且他現在還帶在身上。不到一週前我還看到他用過。」

　　厄特森先生深深地嘆了口氣，一言不發。年輕的恩菲爾先生繼續說道，「這是另一個教訓，沉默是金。我對自己的長舌感到羞愧，我們就此說定，再也不提這事吧。」

　　「我打從心底贊成。就這麼說定了，理查」那位律師附和
地說。

Chapter

寻找海德先生

02

噢，我可憐的老友亨利傑寇爾啊，
如果我曾看過撒旦的臉，那就一定長得跟你的新朋友一樣吧。

　　當天晚上，厄特森先生帶著沉重的心情回到他的單身公寓。他坐在晚餐桌前，食不知味。他一直都習慣在週日晚餐後坐到壁爐旁，讀著生硬艱澀的神學作品，然後當附近教堂敲響十二點的鐘聲時，帶著沉靜感激的心上床休息。但今晚，在餐桌收拾乾淨後，他立即拿起一根蠟燭走進辦公室，接著打開保險箱，從裡頭最隱密的角落，拿出了一份署名為「傑寇爾醫生遺囑」的信封。他眉頭深鎖地研讀它的內容。這份手寫遺囑雖在厄特森先生手中，但當初在撰寫遺囑時他拒絕提供任何協助。遺囑的內容不僅規定亨利傑寇爾醫學博士／民法博士／法律博士／皇家學會會員在去世後，把他的所有財產轉移到「他的朋友兼恩人」愛德華海德名下。同時，若傑寇爾醫生無故失蹤超過三個月，愛德華海德除了支付博士家人一些小額費用外，可免除所有責任與義務，立即承襲亨利傑寇爾的身分地位。此份不切實際的文件，讓熱愛理智和規律生活的厄特森律師頭疼不已。在還不了解遺囑裡的海德先生時，他已經十分憤慨。但現在情況急轉直下，他終於對這個人有了一點了解。之前，當海德只是一個名字時，情況已經夠糟了，而現在這個名字還和一些可怕的事件有關。突然之間，那些曾在眼前的迷霧散去，而在眼前浮現的是一個可怕的惡魔。

　　「我本以為這只是一個瘋狂的舉動。」他邊說邊把那個惱人的文件放回保險箱裡，「但現在我擔心它和不名譽的事扯上關係了」。

　　他話一說完就吹熄蠟燭，穿上大衣，往卡文迪許廣場的方向出發，那裡有許多醫療機構。他有一位受人敬重，且有無數病患的朋友，藍恩醫生住在那。「如果有人知道箇中來由，那必定會是藍恩」他如此想著。

態度莊重的管家熱情招呼他，讓他不用等待就直接進入餐廳，藍恩醫生就坐在酒桌前獨飲。這位衣冠楚楚的紳士面色紅潤，身體健康，態度爽朗果決，雖正值壯年，但已有一頭白髮。他一看到厄特森先生就從椅子上跳起，舉起雙手熱烈歡迎。這種舉止看似過於誇張，但其中蘊含真摯的情誼，因他們兩人已是相識多年的老友，同窗情誼深厚。他們互敬互愛，而且非常享受彼此的陪伴。

一陣閒聊之後，那位律師終於提起盤旋在心中已久的疑問。

「藍恩，我想我們二人應該是亨利傑寇爾最老的朋友吧？」他說。

「我希望能有更年輕的朋友，」藍恩醫生笑著說。「但沒錯，我們是相識最久的朋友，怎麼了？我現在很少跟他聯絡了。」

「真的嗎？我以為你們有共同的興趣。」厄特森回答

「曾經是這樣沒錯，但那都是十幾年前的事了。後來他的那些幻想變得越來越偏激，當然看在過往的交情上我還是關心他，但也就很少跟他碰面了。我沒辦法接受他那些不科學的胡言亂語。」那位醫生說著，激動到臉色發紫。

醫生的慍怒反而讓律師感到寬慰。厄特森是一位對科學毫無熱情的人，他心想，「他們只是在科學方面上有些意見不合。」甚至還加了一句，「這不過就是件小事罷了！」。等他朋友的情緒緩和後，他繼續問，「你有沒有聽過他的一位後輩，叫海德的人？」

「海德？」藍恩重複這個名字「沒有，我從沒聽過。」

這是律師此行獲得的唯一訊息。他當晚在巨大而黑暗的床上翻來覆去，翻騰的思緒在黑暗中掙扎，被無數的問題包圍，直到早晨來臨。

當住處附近的教堂敲響第六聲鐘響時，厄特森先生仍在琢磨這個問題。於此之前，這個問題僅觸及到他理性的那面，但現在他的想像力也被牽扯進來，更確切地說是被控制住了。當他躺在窗簾放下，漆黑一片的房間裡翻來覆去時，恩菲爾先生的故事在他腦海中如同照片一張張接連呈現。他看到晚間城市的一片燈光；然後是一個快速疾行的人；接著一個孩子從醫生的辦公室跑出；然後兩人撞成一團，小孩被那個像貨車一樣前進的人推倒輾過，他不顧她的尖叫踩上她的身體。又或者，他會看到一個富裕家庭的房間，他的朋友在裡頭沉睡，微笑地做著美夢；然後有人打開房間的門，拉開床帳，叫醒他的朋友。瞧！一個渾身都是力量的人站在他身邊，即便在那個死寂的時刻，他也必須起身履行命令。在這兩個場景中出現的人，整晚都在律師的腦海中陰魂不散。即便他打了瞌睡，依舊能看到那人更為鬼祟地穿越沉睡的房屋，或用快速到讓人頭暈的速度，走過城市街燈組成的寬闊迷宮，然後在每個街角撞倒孩子，留下他們獨自尖叫。這個人在夢中沒有面孔，也未幻化出讓人困惑的輪廓，然後就在眼前消失。因此，律師心中迅速滋長出一種對海德先生樣貌的異常好奇心。他想著如果能看到海德一眼，或許就能解開這個謎底，然後放下心中的疑惑。也或許就能理解他朋友的執著，或是鑽牛角尖的原因（隨你怎麼說），也能明白遺囑中那奇異的條款。至少，那會是一張值得一探的臉，一張沒有憐憫心的臉，一張讓一貫冷靜自持的恩菲爾先生，都深惡痛絕的臉。

　　從那時起，厄特森先生就開始在商店街的那道門前徘徊。不管是上班前的早晨，生意繁忙的午間，又或在霧氣籠罩的城市月光下。不管是人潮眾多或稀疏之時，律師總會在他選定的位子上出現。

　　「如果他是海德先生，」他曾想，「那我就是『尋找』先生了」。

　　最終，他的耐心獲得了回報。那是個晴朗乾燥的夜晚，空氣中飄著薄薄的霧氣，街道像舞廳地板一樣乾淨，穩定的光源映照出規律的光影圖案。到了晚上十點，商店已經打烊，小巷人煙稀少，即便倫敦發出的低沉聲響從四面八方傳來，但周遭仍舊非常安靜。街道兩旁傳出的家戶聲響，遠方行人的步行聲，所有細微的聲音都清晰可聞。在老位置站定幾分鐘後，厄特森先生意識到一陣奇異又輕巧的腳步聲。他早已習慣夜間巡邏時被放大的聽覺，使他能清晰地聽見在城市喧嘩聲下的遠處腳步聲。但此次他的注意力份外敏銳集中，所以帶著一股事在必得的強烈預感，他退回院子的入口。

腳步聲越來越近，等快要抵達街道盡頭的轉彎處時，聲音突然變得更大了。律師從入口向外望去，就快要看清楚他的對手是個什麼樣的人。他個子矮小，打扮非常樸素，即便距離那麼遠，他的模樣也讓看到的人心生厭惡。他朝著門口走去，為了節省時間直接穿越馬路；當他靠近時，從口袋中拿出一把鑰匙，就像個要回家的人一樣。

厄特森先生走出來拍了拍他的肩膀說「是海德先生嗎？」

海德先生嚇了一跳，抽了口氣退了一步。但他的恐懼僅維持了一瞬間，隨即恢復冷靜，正眼也沒看那個律師一眼。他冷冷地回答，「是我沒錯。你有什麼事？」

「我看你好像要開門進去。我是傑寇爾的老朋友，住在崗特街的厄特森，你應該有聽過我吧。今天很巧在這裡碰見你，介意我進去坐坐嗎？」律師回答。

「你今天不會見到傑寇爾的，他不在家。」海德先生回答，一邊吹著鎖匙，然後頭也沒抬，突然問道「你怎麼知道我是誰？」

「那你能幫我一個忙嗎？」厄特森先生說

「當然，什麼忙？」他回答

「能讓我看一下你的臉嗎？」律師問

海德先生一開始有些遲疑，但他想了一會兒，然後帶著挑釁的神情抬起頭直視了律師幾秒。「現在我認得出你了，這在未來會有的。」厄特森先生說

「沒錯，我們能碰面是件好事。對了，順帶一提，這是我的地址」海德說了一個蘇活區的門牌號碼。

「天啊！」厄特森先生心想，「他是不是也在想著遺囑的事？」但他沒把心情表露出來，只在接過地址時發出應和的聲音。

「換你告訴我，你是怎麼認出我的？」那個男人說

「有人跟我提過你」律師回答

「是誰提過我？」

「我們有共同的朋友。」厄特森先生說

「共同朋友，是誰？」海德先生有些嘶啞地回覆

「例如，傑寇爾」律師說

「不可能是他，你說謊。」海德怒氣沖沖地大喊。

「你這樣說不太合適吧。」厄特森先生說

那個男人發出一陣野蠻的笑聲，接著突然打開門鎖，然後就消失在房子裡。

海德先生離開後，律師還站在原地不動，神情不安。然後他慢慢沿著街道移動，每走一兩步就停下來，手摸著額頭，陷入困惑。他邊走邊想的問題難以解決。海德先生矮小又蒼白，有一種畸形的感覺，但又看不出來到底是哪裡不對勁。他的微笑讓人不安，對待律師的態度帶著一股殺氣，卻又有種怯懦和莽撞之感。聲音沙啞低沉，聲線有些破碎。以上這些特質都讓人不悅，但還有其他說不上來的原因，讓厄特森先生對他產生一種無所名狀的恐懼和憎恨。「一定還有其他原因，」這位困惑的先生說。「如果我能找到確切的形容詞，他一定還有其他的問題。上帝保佑我，這個男人幾乎不像人類！是因為他身上有種原始人的感覺嗎？還是就像菲爾博士的故事，就是無來由的讓人厭惡呢？又或者是惡靈現身呢？我想可能是後者，噢，我可憐的老友亨利傑寇爾啊，如果我曾看過撒旦的臉，那就一定長得跟你的新朋友一樣吧。」

走過那條小巷，轉彎後有一個廣場。裡頭那些漂亮的老房子身價不再，現在都已經改成分租的公寓或房間了。那裡有各式各樣的租客，包括地圖繪師、建築師、二流律師，或是一些不知道做什麼生意的代理商。但從角落數過來的第二間房子是個例外，它沒有被分租出去。現在除了從氣窗透出的燈光外，它一片漆黑，但仍可從房子的大門感受到富裕的氛圍和舒適。一位衣著考究的年長僕人打開了門。

「普爾，傑寇爾醫生在嗎？」律師問

　　「讓我去看看，厄特森先生」普爾邊說邊帶他走進一個石板鋪成的舒適大廳。那裡屋頂不高，壁爐的火光明亮且溫暖，還擺設了高級的橡木櫥櫃。

　　「您可以在壁爐旁稍等一會嗎，先生？或是您要在餐廳等候呢？」

　　「在這裡就可以了，謝謝你。」他靠著壁爐旁的圍欄說。他目前獨自等待的大廳是他醫生朋友最喜歡的地方，厄特森自己也常說這是全倫敦最舒適的房間。但今晚他感到渾身不對勁，因為海德的臉在他腦海中揮之不去。他感到噁心又沮喪（這可不常在他身上發生）。因為他的低落情緒，櫥櫃上反射的跳動火光似乎也在訴說著危險，連屋頂的影子也讓人感到侷促不安。等普爾回來告訴他傑寇爾醫生不在家時，他因為自己鬆了一口氣而感到羞恥。

　　「普爾，我看到海德先生進入那間舊的解剖室。」他說，「傑寇爾不在的時候，這樣好嗎？」

　　「沒關係的，厄特森先生。海德先生有鎖匙。」僕人回答。

　　「普爾，你的主人好像很信任那位年輕人」律師沉思地回應。

　　「沒錯，的確是這樣。主人告誡我們要聽他的命令。」普爾回答。

「我從沒見過海德先生，對吧？」厄特森問

「當然沒有先生，他從未在這裡用餐。」管家回答，「我們很少在這裡見到他。他大多從實驗室那個門出入。」

「好的，那麼晚安了，普爾。」

「晚安，厄特森先生。」

律師帶著沉重的心踏上回家的路。「可憐的亨利傑寇爾，」他想，「我擔心他有大麻煩了！他應該是年輕時犯了錯，必定是很久之前。但上帝的律法是不會管你是在何時犯錯的。沒錯，一定是這樣。很久以前犯下的罪行，見不得光的恥辱，等到遺忘多年又自我寬恕後才終於出現的懲罰。」律師因為這樣的想法而感到恐懼，細細地思索了自己的過去，深怕在回憶的角落裡也藏有像這樣的滔天大錯。但他的過往可說是無懈可擊，很少人能像他這樣在自我檢視卻不感到憂慮。他為自己曾犯下的錯感到謙卑，同時也滿懷感恩，他曾多次在犯下大錯之前踩了煞車。接著他回到之前的話題，心中生出一絲希望。他想，「如果我能多調查一下這位海德先生。他一定有自己的祕密，看他的樣子，必定是見不得光的祕密。可憐的傑寇爾和他相比，狀況一定不算什麼。事情不能繼續這樣下去。一想到這個人像小偷一樣潛伏在亨利的床邊，我就感到全身發寒。可憐的亨利，你的處境是多麼危險啊！如果海德知道遺囑的存在，他可能會迫不及待地想要繼承財產。如果傑寇爾不阻止我的話，對，我一定要盡力而為。」他補充，「只要傑寇爾願意。」他再次在心中清晰地看到遺囑中那奇怪的條款。

Chapter

傑寇爾醫生神色自若

03

我完全相信你，如果我有得選的話，
你會是我全世界最信任的人，甚至超過我自己。

　　兩週後，在幸運之神的眷顧下，醫生舉行了一場愉快的晚宴。他邀請了五六位老友參加，他們每位都是名聲良好的知識份子，也都熱愛美酒。在其他人都離開後，厄特森先生不動聲色地讓自己留了下來。他不需要特別找什麼藉口，因為這已是常態了。厄特森很討人喜歡，當那些愉悅又多話的賓客們踏出門口時，主人們都喜歡讓這位幹練的律師留晚一點。他們喜歡跟他沉默地坐在一起，讓心情慢慢沉澱，回歸平靜。傑寇爾醫生也不例外，這個身材高大，臉部光滑的五十歲男子坐在壁爐的對面。他的氣質或許有些狡詐，但為人精明善良，也看得出來他真心喜愛厄特森先生。

　　「我一直想要跟你談談，傑寇爾。你記得那份遺囑嗎？」厄特森先生說。

　　旁人也許會意識到這不是個輕鬆的話題，但醫生卻雲淡風輕地回答：「我可憐的老友厄特森，你手上有一個這麼棘手的客戶。除了那個迂腐的老頑固藍恩，我沒想到你會被那份遺囑如此困擾。他認為我的科學是異端邪說。喔，我知道他是一個好人，你不用皺眉，我也想跟他保持交情，但他就是一個迂腐又無知的老學究，我對他非常失望。

　　「你知道我從不贊成你立的那份遺囑，」厄特森接著說，沒有跟著轉移話題。

　　「我的遺囑？當然，我知道。你告訴過我了。」醫生尖銳地回答。

　　「我要再強調一次，」律師接著說，「因為我對那位年輕的海德先生有了更深的了解。」

傑寇爾醫生英挺的臉變得蒼白，眼神變得幽暗。「不要再說了，我以為我們已經說好，不再提及此事」他說。

「海德先生的事非常可怕。」厄特森說

「這不會改變任何事，你不了解我的立場。」醫生的態度有些轉變。「厄特森，我的處境艱難，事實上是非常糟糕。就算是說出來也不會有任何幫助的。」

「傑寇爾，你知道的，你可以信任我。說出實情，我保證我可以幫你脫身。」

「我的好朋友厄特森，」醫生說，「你真是個天大的好人，我沒辦法用言語表達我的感謝之情。我完全相信你，如果我有得選的話，你會是我全世界最信任的人，甚至超過我自己。但事情不像你想得那麼糟，如果能讓你安心的話，我在此向你保證，只要我想要，我現在就能擺脫海德先生。真的非常謝謝你這麼擔心我。我只想再多說一句，我相信你會聽進去的。厄特森，這是我的隱私，希望你以後不要再提了。」

厄特森看著爐火想了一會兒。

「我相信你一定會做正確的決定。」他邊說邊站起身。

「希望這是我們最後一次談到這件事，但既然我們已經在這個話題上，」醫生繼續說，「我希望你能明白，我真的非常關心可憐的海德先生。我知道你跟他碰過面，他和我說了。我猜他有點無禮，但我真的非常關心那位可憐的年輕人。如果哪天我不在了，厄特森希望你能答應我，你會體諒他並且讓他獲得他應得的權利。我知道你一定會做到，但如果我能親耳聽到你答應我，我會放心得多。」

「我沒辦法假裝我喜歡他」律師回答。

「我沒要求你喜歡他，」傑寇爾把手放到律師的手臂上懇切地說，「我只是希望你能主持正義。當我不在的時候，希望你會幫助他。」

厄特森無奈地嘆了一口氣說，「好吧，我答應你。」

Chapter

凱魯謀殺案

04

她看起來不是良善的人，但掩飾得很好，
應對進對非常有禮貌。

　　過了將近一年的時間，十月十八日倫敦發生了一起慘絕人寰的兇殺案，被害者的高社經地位讓整起事件更為引人注目。案件的細節不多卻讓聽者戰慄。有名獨居的女僕，住在離河不遠的房子裡。她當天晚上十一點上樓休息。儘管霧氣在凌晨時籠罩了整座城市，但那天稍早時萬里無雲，女僕房間俯瞰的小巷被月光照亮。她似乎是個相當浪漫的人，因為當晚她坐在窗台邊的箱子上時，立刻做起了白日夢。她說她從未感到如此平和，並覺得世界非常美妙（她描述事情發生經過時，眼淚洶湧而出）。她看到一位滿頭白髮的年長男士走進小巷，要與另一位身材矮小的男士會面，一開始她並未注意到那位矮小的先生。他們開始交談後（就在那位女僕的眼前），年長的男士鞠了躬，非常禮貌地和對方說話。他的動作看起來像在問路而已，談話的內容感覺不太重要。女僕欣賞地看著他被月光照亮的臉，那神情透露著純真和年長的善良氣息，又帶著一絲的高貴自信。

　　然後她轉向看往另一位男士，非常驚訝地發現他是一位叫海德的人。他之前曾經拜訪過她的主人，她當時對他就沒有好感。他手中把玩著一根沉重的手杖，一言不發，不耐煩地聽著老紳士說話。接著他突然發怒，一邊用力跺腳，一邊揮舞手杖，就像個瘋子一樣（女僕使用的形容詞）。那位年長的男人驚訝地退了一步，像是被對方侮辱一樣。下個瞬間，海德就把被害人打倒在地，像一隻憤怒的猿猴，又踢又踹，對那個人施以毒打，骨頭斷裂的聲音都清晰可聞。老先生的身體倒在路上抽搐，而這個可怕的場景讓女僕嚇得暈了過去。

　　她凌晨兩點恢復意識報了警。兇手早就已經離開，而受害者躺在小巷中央，不成人形。拿來打人的手杖雖然堅固又厚重，但已經從中斷成兩截，其中一半滾進了附近的排水溝裡，另一半則毫無疑問被兇手帶走了。從受害者的身上找到一個皮夾和金手錶，除了一個已經封好且蓋有郵戳的信封外，沒有任何卡片或文件。看來他是準備寄出那個寫著厄特森姓名和住址的信封。

隔天早上，那位律師還沒起床就被這件事叫醒。他聽到事件後嘴唇緊閉，神情嚴肅地說「沒看到屍體前我不會發表評論，情況可能非常嚴重。請等我穿好衣服。」他帶著嚴肅的心情快速用完早餐，然後駕著馬車去警局，屍體已經送到那了。他一進入房間就點頭說，「是的，我認得他。非常遺憾，這位是丹佛凱魯。」

「天啊，老天！這不會是真的吧？」警官驚呼，眼裡帶著破案的決心。「這齣案件會引起民眾的關注，或許你能幫我們找到兇手。」接著，他簡短地敘述了女僕的證詞，並給他看那根斷裂的手杖。

厄特森先生本已對海德這個名字感到恐懼，當他看到斷裂的手杖時，他再也沒有懷疑了。那手杖就是他多年前送給亨利傑寇爾的禮物。

「那位海德先生是否身形矮小？」他問

「非常矮小而且外型猥瑣，那位女僕是這樣說的。」警官回答

厄特森先生想了想然後抬起頭，「請跟我來，我可以帶你去他的住處。」

此時大約是早上九點，是本季的第一場霧。一片巨大的深色雲霧籠罩著天空，風呼呼地吹，霧氣忽濃忽淡。馬車在巷弄間穿梭時，厄特森先生看到各式色調的曙光，有時如同夜晚般漆黑，有時則是濃郁的紅棕色，就像場猛烈的火光。有時，霧氣被稍稍吹散，一絲微弱的天光就從縫隙中照了下來。這慘澹的蘇活街區，不斷變化的光影，泥濘的街道，邋遢的行人，為了抵擋黑暗而重新點燃（或從未熄滅）的街燈，都讓這位律師覺得這裡就像惡夢裡的城市，讓他內心的想法也變得黑暗起來。當他望向同行的夥伴時，他感到對法律和執法者的害怕，這種恐懼的情緒連那些最誠實正直的人都無法倖免。

當馬車抵達那個地址時，霧氣已些微散去。他們看到的那條陰暗街道上有著破舊的酒吧，低檔的法國餐館，賣著便宜吃食的小吃店。每家商店門口都擠著許多衣著破爛的孩子，不同國籍的婦女來來去去，她們手上拿著鑰匙，走出來門來喝上一杯。下一刻，霧又濃了，掩蓋了所有的東西，就像棕色的土一樣，把他和那些粗鄙的背景分隔開來。亨利傑寇爾選中的繼承人就住在這，他將擁有 25 萬英鎊的財產。

一位臉色蠟黃，頭髮銀白的老婦人開了門。她看起來不是良善的人，但掩飾得很好，應對進對非常有禮貌。她說，是的，這是海德先生的住所，但他現在不在家。他昨晚很晚才到家，但待不到一小時就又離開了，因為他的作息很不規律，所以這很常發生。比方說，除了昨晚，她已經幾乎兩個月沒見到他了。

「很好，現在我們想看看他的房間。」律師說。在那個婦人開口拒絕時，他接著說，「我和你介紹一下，這位是倫敦警局的紐康門警官。」

那婦人的臉上閃過一絲幸災樂禍的神情。她說「喔！他闖禍了，他做了什麼？」

厄特森和警官互看了一眼。「看得出來他不怎麼討人喜歡。」警官說，「現在請讓我們去查看一下吧。」

整棟房子除了老婦人外空無一人。海德先生雖然只用了兩間房，但裡頭裝飾都十分豪華高雅。櫥櫃裡放滿了葡萄酒，還有銀製的餐具，優雅的桌布。牆上也掛著精美的畫作。厄特森猜想是亨利傑寇爾送給他的禮物，因為亨利是一位優秀的鑑賞家。地板上也鋪了多層的地毯，顏色非常和諧。但這兩間房都十分凌亂，看得出來最近被匆忙地翻找過。衣服都堆在地上，口袋被翻了出來，上鎖的抽屜是開著的，壁爐裡有一層厚厚的灰，感覺燒了很多文件。在這堆灰燼中，警官找到一本還沒被火燒完的綠色支票簿，而那斷掉的半根手杖則在門後找到。隨後，他們前往銀行，發現兇手的帳戶裡有幾千磅的存款，這所有的證據都讓警官非常滿意。

他告訴厄特森先生，「你可以放心了，先生，他跑不掉了。他一定很慌張，不然不會把那半根手杖放在那，或燒掉自己的支票簿。錢對人來說非常重要。我們現在要做的就是在銀行等他出現，然後發佈追緝令。」

但發布追緝令一點都不容易，因為海德沒有什麼熟識的朋友，即便是女管家也只見過他兩次。更沒有辦法追蹤到他的家人，他從未拍過照，而能夠形容他長相的人，描述的內容大相逕庭。大家共通的感想只有一點，那就是這個逃犯給人一種說不上來的畸形感，讓每個人都印象深刻。

Chapter

海德的信箋

05

沉睡的霧氣仍然籠罩在城市上方，
路上的街燈像寶石一樣閃閃發亮，在低矮的雲霧下，
城鎮中的日子仍舊向前滾動，像強風一樣發出了聲響。

厄特森先生在那天午後傍晚時分，抵達傑寇爾醫生的家。普爾立刻讓他進門，領著他穿過廚房，走過花園改建的庭院，進入俗稱實驗室或是解剖室的建築物裡。傑寇爾醫生跟另一位外科醫生的繼承人買下了這棟房子。和解剖學相比，傑寇爾醫生對化學比較有興趣，所以改建了花園裡這個建物。這是律師第一次進入這棟房子的這一區。他好奇地看著這個陰暗無窗的建築，環顧四周，感到一種不尋常的排斥感。他穿過那手術室，過去曾經擠滿熱切學生，現在卻荒涼寂靜，桌上擺滿了化學器具，地板上散落著木箱和打包用的乾草，昏暗的光線透過霧濛濛的圓頂照了下來。在另一頭，有道樓梯通往一扇紅色襯墊的大門，穿過這扇門，厄特森先生終於進入醫生的房間。這個房間很大，裡頭有數個玻璃櫥櫃，一面全身鏡跟一張辦公桌，還有三扇布滿灰塵的鐵窗能看到外頭的庭院。壁爐裡生著火，煙囪的架子上放著一盞燈，即便在房子裡，霧氣也變得十分濃厚。傑寇爾醫生坐在靠近火堆的溫暖地方，他看起來生了重病，非常虛弱。他沒有站起身歡迎客人，僅伸出冰涼的手，用變調的聲音迎接他。

普爾一離開後，厄特森就立刻說「你聽說發生的事了嗎？」

醫生打了個冷顫，「我在餐廳時就聽到他們在廣場大聲吆喝了。」

「一件事，」律師說，「凱魯是我的客戶，但你也是。我想搞清楚我在幹嘛。你應該沒有瘋到窩藏這個逃犯吧？」

　　「厄特森，我對天發誓。」醫生大喊，「我發誓絕不會再跟他碰面。我以名譽發誓，從此不會跟他有任何牽扯。一切都結束了，而且沒錯他不要我的幫忙，我非常了解他。記住我的話，他現在很安全，也絕對不會再出現了。」

　　律師不悅地聽著他朋友激動的言行。「你聽起來很篤定，為了你好，我希望你是對的。如果要上法院的話，你的名字可能會牽連其中。」

　　「基於某種理由我無法跟任何人說明，但我非常確定。」傑寇爾回答，「但有件事我需要你的意見。我收到一封信，我不太確定是否應該交給警方。我希望你能說說你的想法，厄特森。我相信你會給我聰明的建議，你是我最信任的人。」

　　「我猜你是擔心這會暴露他的行蹤？」律師問

　　「不，我一點都不關心海德的下場。我和他已經一刀兩斷了，我是擔心我自己，這件事可能會讓我的名譽受損。」

　　厄特森沉默了一會，對自己朋友的自私感到驚訝，但又鬆了一口氣。「那麼，讓我看一下那封信吧。」他最後說。

　　這封信的署名是「愛德華海德」，裡頭是一種奇怪的直立手寫體。信中簡短地說，他愧對他的恩人－傑寇爾醫生過往的種種恩情，請傑寇爾不要替他的安危操心，他已找到可靠的逃亡方式。律師對這封信的內容非常滿意，因為裡頭證實了他倆之間的關係不如他想像中的糟糕。他也因為自己以前曾有的懷疑而感到羞愧。

「你還留著信封嗎？」他問

「我把信封燒了，」傑寇爾回答，「我沒想清楚就燒了，但上頭沒有郵戳。這封信是直接送到家的。」

「我可以留著這封信，然後明天再回覆你嗎？」厄特森問

「我希望你幫我處理這件事，我已經對自己的判斷失去信心了。」醫生回答。

「我會想想，」律師回答，「另一件事，你遺囑裡提到有關失蹤那條款，是海德的主意？」

醫生看起來像是要昏倒了一樣，緊閉著嘴巴，點了點頭。

「我就知道！」厄特森說，「他想謀殺你，你幸運逃過一劫了。」

「我已經學到教訓了，」醫生嚴肅地回答，「天啊，厄特森，我真的嘗到苦果了！」他用手搗著臉說。

律師在離開時，問了普爾，「對了，今天有封信送到這裡來。你還記得送信的人長什麼樣子嗎？」但普爾非常確定今天除了郵差之外，沒人送來任何東西，「而且都只是一些垃圾郵件罷了。」

這個消息讓律師害怕了起來。顯而易見地，這封信是送到實驗室門口的，甚至有可能是在辦公室裡寫的。如果真是如此，就得用不同的角度來判斷，還得更加小心謹慎。派報小童們在路邊大聲地嘶吼，「快報！國會議員謀殺案！」這是他朋

友和客戶的喪禮致詞，而他不得不擔心另一位好友的名聲也會被捲入這場醜聞之中。這是個很艱難的決定，即便他習慣靠自己解決問題，但也開始希望尋求他人的建議。他不能直接去問別人的意見，但或許可以旁敲側擊來進行。

不久後，他坐在家裡的壁爐旁，對面則是他的首席職員，葛斯特先生。他們中間擺著一瓶在他家地下室收藏多年的陳年好酒。沉睡的霧氣仍然籠罩在城市上方，路上的街燈像寶石一樣閃閃發亮，在低矮的雲霧下，城鎮中的日子仍舊向前滾動，像強風一樣發出了聲響。在火光映照下的房間裡氣氛歡快，酒中的酸味早已消失，酒色也隨著時光的流逝而變得柔和，如同穿過彩繪玻璃而變得濃烈的光線。秋日午後的陽光照在山坡上的葡萄園，準備驅散倫敦的霧氣。律師的心情在不知不覺中放鬆了。他總懷疑自己是否在無意間洩露了太多秘密，葛斯特先生是最了解他的人。他也因為工作關係常到醫生那去，也認識普爾，不可能不知道海德先生能夠在房子裡自由進出的事。他或許已經推論出事情的原委了，如果能讀一下那封可以解開謎團的信不是更好嗎？況且，葛斯特對於字跡頗有研究，相信也能理解這是個合情合理的作法。除此之外，葛斯特先生相當擅長提供建議，他看到這麼奇怪的信一定會有些想法，厄特森先生也能依此決定未來該怎麼做。

「發生在丹佛先生身上的事真的太不幸了。」他說

「沒錯。這件事讓民眾都憤憤不平，那個兇手毫無疑問是瘋了。」葛斯特回答。

「我想聽聽你的意見。」厄特森回答「我這裡有封兇手親手寫的信，請保守秘密，因為我實在不知道該如何是好。這件事真是不能再糟了。信在這裡，這是兇手的筆跡。」

葛斯特的眼睛睜大，立刻熱切地讀起那封信。「先生，我覺得他沒有瘋。但這人的字跡很奇異。」

「是個怪人寫的。」律師繼續說

接著有個僕人進房，遞給律師一張紙條。

「先生，那是傑寇爾先生的字條嗎？」職員說，「我認得出他的筆跡。厄特森先生，有什麼不好說的事嗎？」

「只是個晚宴的邀請函。為什麼這麼問？你想看看嗎？」

「謝謝你先生，請讓我看看。」然後他把兩張紙並排放在桌上，開始細看比對內容。「好了先生，這筆跡非常有趣。」他看完後把兩封信還給厄特森。

之後他們倆人陷入沉默，厄特森先生有些不安，最後突然問到，「葛斯特，你為什麼要比較這兩份筆跡？」

「先生，因為這兩份筆跡有些相似，很多地方都完全一樣，只是角度有些不同。」

「這就奇怪了」厄特森說。

「沒錯，的確很奇怪」葛斯特回答。

「我不希望別人知道這件事。」律師說

「那是當然，我了解」職員回答

當晚，厄特森趁沒人注意的時候把那張字條永遠鎖到保險箱裡。他想著，「到底是怎麼回事？亨利傑寇爾竟然幫一個兇手偽造文書！」這個想法讓他渾身發冷。

Chapter

藍恩醫生遇到的奇事

06

我坐在長椅上曬著太陽，體內的獸性蠢蠢欲動，靈魂仍似睡非睡，
想著要繼續懺悔贖罪，但還未開始進行。

　　時光飛逝，丹佛爵士的死被視為對社會大眾的攻擊，所以懸賞海德的金額高達數千英磅，但他卻像是從未出現過一樣，人間蒸發。他不堪的過去被揭露出來，都是一些殘忍無情的故事，還有他邪惡的生活，奇怪的交友圈，以及職業圈中的招來的仇恨敵意。但他現在的下落卻毫無聲息。從謀殺的那天早上離開蘇活區的住所後，他彷彿像被抹去了一樣。隨著時間推移，厄特森先生也逐漸從驚恐中恢復，回到他原本平靜的生活。在他看來，海德的消失是丹佛爵士死亡的回報。而現在，因為邪惡的影響消失，傑寇爾醫生開始了新的生活。他遠離了隱居的日子，重新和朋友們聯繫，再度成為他們熟知的客人和主人。他以前因為從事各項慈善事業而聞名，現在對宗教活動也相當虔誠。他十分忙碌，經常露面做善事，看起來既明亮又寬廣，彷彿有種發自內心的服務熱忱。超過兩個月的時間，那位醫生過著平靜的日子。

　　一月八號那天，厄特森前往醫生家享用晚餐，當晚藍恩也在受邀行列內。那晚醫生對待他們的方式就和從前一樣，當時他們三人還是非常要好的朋友。但到了十二和十四號，律師吃了閉門羹。普爾說「醫生把自己關在房子裡，不願接見任何客人」。十五號，他又再度登門拜訪，但仍被拒絕。厄特森過去兩個月幾乎天天都跟傑寇爾碰面，現在醫生又回到之前避不見面的狀態，律師開始擔心起來。第五天，他跟葛斯特用餐，次日去了藍恩家拜訪。

　　至少在藍恩家他沒有被拒於門外，但在進屋後，他驚愕地發現醫生的外貌變了很多。死神在他臉上做了記號，原本紅潤的雙頰變得蒼白，體重減輕，掉髮嚴重而且顯得十分衰老。但引起律師注意的並非這些肉體上的變化。醫生眼神中的擔憂，還有行為舉止間流露出的恐懼反而更引人注目。雖然厄特森認為身為一位醫生應該不會害怕死亡，但他還是沒辦法肯定。他心想，「對，身為一位醫生，他必定知道自己已經來日不多，但應該還是難以接受這個消息。」不過當厄特森提到藍恩看起來狀況不太好時，醫生對自己即將死亡一事非常確定。

「我受到極大的打擊，而且已經無法恢復了，我只剩下幾週的時間。不過，我有個很美好的人生，也過得非常開心。沒錯，我曾經很熱愛生命，但有時我會想，如果我們什麼都懂的話，或許死亡也不是什麼大不了的事。」

「傑寇爾也病了。你有見過他嗎？」厄特森說

藍恩的臉色大變，他舉起顫抖的手說，「我再也不想看到或聽到有關傑寇爾醫生的事。我不想跟那個人有任何瓜葛，也希望你也不要再提到他，我就當他已經死了。」他用顫抖的聲音大聲說。

「這…有什麼我能做的事嗎？」厄特森先生停頓了一會兒說，「我們三人是認識很久的老朋友了，藍恩，這輩子不會再有這種朋友了。」

藍恩回答「你什麼都沒辦法做，你可以去問他。」

「他不願意見我。」律師回答

「我一點都不驚訝，厄特森。等我死後的某天，也許你就

會知道誰對誰錯，我沒辦法告訴你。現在，請你看在上天的份上，坐下跟我聊聊其他的事吧。但如果你沒辦法不管這事，那拜託，就走吧，我沒辦法忍受。」藍恩回答。

　　他一到家就坐下寫信給傑寇爾，抱怨自己被拒於門外，並詢問他和藍恩鬧翻的原因。隔天，他收到一封長長的回信，措辭十分悲傷，但有時又神祕地含糊不清。和藍恩的紛爭是無法解決的，「我不會怪我們的老友，」傑寇爾寫道，「但我同意他的想法，我們不該繼續來往。從現在起，我要進入極度隱居的生活。如果你常常被拒於門外，請不要感到驚訝，或是懷疑我們的友誼。你必須讓我踏上屬於自己的黑暗之途，我加諸在自己身上的懲罰是危險和無法言喻的。如果我是罪人之首，我也是痛苦之首。我無法想像世界上會有個地方讓人如此受到折磨和恐懼，厄特森，你現在唯一能為我做的事就是尊重我的靜默。」厄特森非常驚訝。海德之前所帶來的邪惡影響已經消退，醫生也回到他原來的日常生活和交友圈。僅僅一週前，未來還充滿了歡笑和光輝，但現在友誼、平靜的心和生活都被瞬間摧毀。只有瘋狂才會造成這樣巨大而且意外的改變，但從藍恩的言行舉止看來，其中必定有更深的理由。

　　一週後藍恩臥病在床，不到兩週的時間就去世了。葬禮結束後的當晚，心情悲傷的厄特森把辦公室門鎖上，憂鬱地坐在燭火旁，拿出一封他已故朋友親筆寫下和密封的信件。上頭寫著「私人：僅供 G.J. 厄特森個人閱讀。若他去世，直接銷毀，不可打開。」信封上的特別說明讓律師非常害怕裡頭的內容。「我今天已經埋葬了一個朋友，如果這封信會讓我失去另一個朋友呢？」他想著。但他譴責自己這種不忠誠的想法，於是打開了信封。裡頭還有另一個信封，一樣是密封狀態，上頭寫著「若亨利傑寇爾去世或失蹤才可打開。」厄特森不敢相信自己的眼睛，沒錯，這裡也寫著失蹤，就像是他還給傑寇爾的那份瘋狂的遺囑一樣。失蹤和亨利傑寇爾的名字又同時出現了。在那份遺囑裡，邪惡的海德是出主意的人，他的目的非常清楚又可怕。但藍恩親筆寫的，又是什麼意思呢？厄特森燃起了好奇心，想要無視禁令直接打開信封一探究竟。但是他不可破壞身為律師的職業操守以及對朋友的忠誠，所以他又把這封信放到他私人保險箱的深處。

克制和戰勝好奇心是兩回事，而自第四天起，律師也不再如此執著於他那仍活著的朋友了。他的思念之情依舊，但其中夾帶了些許不安和恐懼。他仍舊試著前往拜訪，但在被拒絕入內時鬆了口氣。也許在內心深處，他寧願在流通的空氣和充滿城市聲響的空間下，站在門口和普爾說話。而不是進入房子，和那位自願軟禁的神祕隱士交談。普爾也的確沒什麼愉快的消息可以轉達。據說那位醫生越來越常待在實驗室上方的房間裡，有時甚至睡在那。他情緒低落，變得非常沉默，也停止閱讀，感覺心事重重。厄特森對於這些消息越來越習以為常，也漸漸不再前往拜訪了。

Chapter

窗邊事件

07

故事終於畫上句點了，我們再也不會看到海德先生了。

又到了厄特森和恩菲爾固定散步的週日時間。他們走過那條小巷,在經過那扇大門時,兩人不約而同地停下了腳步。

「故事終於畫上句點了,我們再也不會看到海德先生了。」恩菲爾說。

「我也希望如此。我之前有跟你提過曾見過他一次嗎?那時我也和你一樣有那種厭惡噁心的感覺。」厄特森說

「只要看到他,一定會有那種感覺的。」恩菲爾回答。「而且你是不是覺得我很愚蠢,竟然不知道這扇門是傑寇爾醫生家的後門。事實上我會發現這件事也是因為你的關係。」

「你也發現了,是嗎?」厄特森說,「如果是這樣的話,我們可以走到院子裡看看窗戶。老實說,我有點放不下可憐的傑寇爾,就算我們只是在外頭看一眼,我想看到朋友的出現也會對他有點幫助。」

雖然頭上的天空在夕陽餘暉下依舊十分明亮,但院子裡十分陰冷,也有些昏暗。三扇窗中,有一扇窗半開著,傑寇爾醫生就坐在旁邊透氣。他看來神情十分悲傷,像是一個被關起來的囚犯。

「嘿!傑寇爾,」他大喊,「我想你應該覺得好多了吧!」

「我狀況很糟,厄特森。」傑寇爾醫生沉悶地說,「非常不好,但是感謝老天,這狀況不會維持太久。」

律師說,「你不該把自己關在室內,應該要多出門走動。

就像我跟恩菲爾先生一樣，走一走刺激循環。(這是我的親戚，恩菲爾先生，這是傑寇爾醫生)。快點帶著你的帽子出來，跟我們活動活動。」

「謝謝你的邀請，」傑寇爾嘆了口氣。「我非常想出去，但是沒辦法，我不敢出門。不過厄特森，我真的非常高興能見到你。如果可以，我會邀請你和恩菲爾先生進門坐坐，只可惜這地方實在無法接待客人。」

「那現在，」律師和氣地說，「最好的辦法就是我們在這院子裡跟你說說話了。」

「這也是我想建議的方式」，醫生帶著微笑回答。但這句話剛說出口，他臉上的微笑就被一種絕望和極度恐懼的神情所取代，這一瞬間的轉變足以讓底下倆位紳士的血液凍僵。窗戶立刻被關上，所以他們僅看到一眼，但那一瞬間就已經足夠。他們倆人轉身離開院子一言不發，沉默地走過小巷，直到抵達附近的街區。在那裡即便是週日，也仍舊有些熱鬧的生活痕跡。厄特森先生終於轉身看向他的同伴，他們倆都臉色蒼白，眼中有著相同的恐懼。

「願上天寬恕我們。」厄特森說

但恩菲爾先生僅神情嚴肅地點了點頭，接著沉默地走開。

Chapter

最後一晚

08

我知道大家都非常焦躁不安，
我們現在就是要讓一切畫上句點。

某天晚餐後，厄特森先生坐在壁爐旁時，普爾突然到訪。

「普爾，你怎麼會來？」他喊道，然後再看了普爾一眼「發生什麼事了？醫生病了嗎？」他接著說

「厄特森先生，事情不太對勁」普爾說

「快坐下，這杯酒給你喝」律師說，「慢慢把事情說清楚。」

「你知道醫生的行事作風，他現在又把自己囚禁在房間裡了。這次，我覺得不太對勁。厄特森先生，我很害怕。」

「我的好朋友，說清楚點。你害怕什麼？」律師說

「我已經擔驚受怕了一個禮拜，再也受不了了。」普爾說，沒有正面回答他的問題。

普爾的話從他的行為舉止裡表露出來，他的神情非常緊張。除了剛開始說他很害怕的那一刻，其他時間他都沒有正眼看過律師。即便是現在，他膝蓋上放著那杯一口也沒碰的紅酒，他的眼睛仍然緊盯著地板上的一個角落，「我再也無法忍受了」他重複說。

「來，普爾，我知道你的擔心一定其來有自。試著告訴我發生了什麼事。」

「我認為發生了嚴重的罪行」普爾沙啞地說

「罪行？」律師大喊出聲，他因為恐懼而變得有些急躁。

「嚴重的罪行？你在說什麼？」

「先生，我不敢說」普爾回答「但你願意跟我來看一看嗎？」

厄特森先生雖然沒有回答，但是起身拿了帽子跟大衣。他也驚訝地發現當管家放下那杯一口都沒喝的酒時，臉上露出了寬慰的神情。

那是一個典型的三月夜晚，荒涼又寒冷。蒼白的月亮像被強風吹倒一樣，斜斜地掛在天際，稀薄的雲層快速地飄動。在強風之下，交談變得困難，臉上也被凍出了紅斑。街上的行人異常稀少，厄特森先生從未見過倫敦的街道如此空曠。他多希望能碰到人群，讓街頭變得再熱鬧一些。儘管心中充滿掙扎，但他有種即將大難臨頭的強烈預感。當他們抵達廣場時，塵土漫天飛舞，花園中瘦長的樹木被強風吹得倒向圍欄。一直走在前頭的普爾，在人行道中間停了下來，儘管寒風刺骨，他脫下了帽子，拿出紅色的手帕擦拭額頭。他的汗水不是因為快步趕路所致，而是因為在某種極端的痛苦之下流出的冷汗。他的臉色發白，說話時的聲音嘶啞又破碎。

「先生，我們到了。希望老天保佑沒有壞事發生。」

「希望如此，普爾」律師說

管家謹慎地敲了們，門開了一條小縫，「是你嗎，普爾？」

「對，是我。快開門」普爾說

他們進入明亮的大廳，壁爐的火生得很旺。所有的僕人，不分男女都站在那裡，像是一群綿羊。一看到厄特森先生，女僕就開始歇斯底里地嗚咽，廚師也大喊出聲「感謝老天，是厄特森先生！」一邊向前跑，像要擁抱他一樣。

「什麼？你們怎麼都在這裡？」律師不高興地說「這成何體統，你們的主人會生氣的。」

「他們都很害怕」普爾說

大廳陷入一片沉默，沒有人抗議。只有女僕開始大聲哭泣。

「安靜！」普爾對她說，自己的聲音也流露出緊張不安的情緒。事實上，當那個女僕突然放聲大哭時，他們都露出恐懼的神色，轉頭看向內門的方向。管家對著刀童說，「現在，拿蠟燭給我，我們立刻把這件事解決。」然後他請求厄特森先生跟著他一起走入後花園。

「先生，現在請你放輕腳步。我希望你能仔細聆聽，但不要被他發現。如果他要求你入內，請你拒絕他。」

厄特森先生被這突如其來的警告嚇到了，腳下一軟差點失去平衡。但他仍舊鼓起勇氣，跟著管家進入實驗室的建築物裡，穿過擺滿箱子罐子的外科手術室，走到階梯底。普爾示意他站在一側仔細傾聽，普爾則放下手上的蠟燭，下定決心鼓足勇氣，爬上樓梯，有些不確定地敲了敲覆蓋著紅絨布的房門。

「先生，厄特森先生希望能見您一面，」他說，同時激動地要律師仔細聽聽房內的動靜。

「跟他說我誰都不見」房內傳來了帶著抱怨語氣的回應。

「好的，先生」普爾回答，聲調中帶著一絲得意。他拿起蠟燭，領著厄特森先生回到院子，走進廚房。此時廚房的爐火已經熄滅，地板上有甲蟲在爬。

「先生，你覺得那是我主人的聲音嗎？」他看著厄特森先生的眼睛說

「和以前相比，變了很多」律師臉色蒼白地看著他回答。

「變了？是的，我也這麼認為」管家說，「我在這裡工作二十年了，不會認不出他的聲音。先生，就在八天前我家主人被殺了。我們聽到他在房裡大叫上帝的名字，然後有人冒名頂替了他，我不知道他為什麼還要留在房間裡，厄特森先生！」

「普爾，這件事太奇怪了，」厄特森咬著指甲說。「就算你說的是真的，傑寇爾醫生真的已經死了，殺手為什麼還要留下來？這完全說不過去，一點都不合理。」

「厄特森先生，你不好說服，但我會向你說明我的理由。」普爾說。「你一定要知道，現在房間裡的那個人或怪物，上週不分日夜地哭喊著要某種藥，但沒辦法確定種類。主人有時會跟我們用紙條溝通。他會在紙上寫下指示，丟到樓梯上叫我們執行。整個星期我們都收到寫在紙條上的指令，房門從來沒有開過，他還會趁沒有人注意的時候才把餐點拿進去。沒錯，先生，我們一整天裡收到兩次或三次的命令跟抱怨。我被派去城

內所有的藥局買藥，但他總是不滿意，叫我去退貨，因為藥的成份不夠純。然後再去別家買藥。不管原因為何，他非常需要這種藥。」

「你手邊還留有他的字條嗎？」厄特森先生問

普爾摸了摸口袋拿出一張皺巴巴的紙條，律師低頭就著燭光仔細檢查。紙條的內容寫著：「本人傑寇爾醫生向莫氏公司的諸位問好。我非常確信上次獲得的藥品成分不純，無法符合我的需求。在18—年時，我曾向貴公司購入一大批藥物，請仔細搜尋，如果手邊仍有同批的藥品，請立刻提供給我，費用不是問題。這件事情對我極度重要。」寫到這裡，紙條的內容還算平常。但接下來，撰寫人的情緒突然崩潰，他接著寫著，「看在老天的份上，找一些舊的藥給我。」

「這張信箋蠻奇怪的，」厄特森先生說，接著尖銳地質問他，「你怎麼把信拆開了？」

「先生，因為莫氏公司的人很生氣。那個人把這張信箋像垃圾一樣丟還給我。」普爾回答。

「你也認為這張信箋一定是醫生寫的，對吧？」律師接著問

「我認為是他寫的沒錯，」僕人悶悶不樂地回答。語氣一轉接著說，「但是誰寫得又如何，我親眼看到他了！」

「看到他？」厄特森先生說，「什麼意思？」

　　「那個人一定是他！」普爾說。「事情是這樣的，那天我突然從花園走進手術室。他看起來像是溜出來在找藥或別的東西，因為房間的門是開著的。他站在手術室的那一頭，埋頭在箱子裡找東西。他抬頭看到我進來，叫了出聲，然後迅速跑上樓回到房間裡。我只看見他不到一分鐘，但我背上的汗毛都豎起來了。如果是主人的話，他為什麼要戴著面具？如果是主人的話，他為什麼要發出像老鼠一樣的叫聲然後逃走呢？我服侍他這麼久的時間了，然後…」他停下來，用手揉了揉臉。

　　厄特森先生說「這些事情都非常奇怪，但我好像有點頭緒了。普爾，你的主人應該是得了讓人飽受折磨，面目變形的疾病。就是這個原因才讓他聲音改變，還需要帶著面具避不見面，並且急需藥物治療，因為他仍然認為還有痊癒的可能。希望上天保佑他！這就是我的想法，普爾，事情演變至此非常不幸。這一切的確都非常嚇人，但這是最合情合理的解釋，我們不要再胡亂揣測了。」

　　「先生，」管家的臉色變得一陣青一陣白，「那個東西不是我家主人，我非常確定。我的主人，」他望了望四周壓低聲音說，「身材高大，而那個東西非常矮小。」厄特森先生想要反駁。「喔，先生，」普爾大喊，「我已經服侍主人二十年了，你以為我認不出來嗎？你認為我不會知道他站起來身高到房門的哪裡嗎？我每天早上都看到他。不，先生，那個戴著面具的東西不是傑寇爾醫生。天知道那是什麼，但絕對不是傑寇爾。我非常肯定他一定被謀殺了。」

　　「普爾，」律師回答，「如果你這麼說，那我的責任就是要確定發生的事。即便我不希望讓你的主人感到尷尬，我也認為那封信箋代表你家主人還活著，但我還是必須盡到責任，破門而入查看了。」

「厄特森先生，這樣做就對了！」管家大喊

「現在，第二個問題是，誰該打破那扇門？」厄特森繼續說

「當然是你跟我了，先生」管家毫不遲疑地回答。

「說的非常好，」律師回答，「不管發生了什麼事，我一定會讓你全身而退的。」

「手術室裡有把斧頭，你可以拿廚房裡的火鉗防身。」普爾繼續說

律師拿起那把粗糙又沉重工具，掂了掂重量。「普爾，你知道我們倆即將以身犯險嗎？」他抬起頭說

「先生，你說的對」管家回答

「那麼我們就該對彼此坦白。」律師接著說，「我們都有些話沒說，就讓我們一吐為快吧。這個帶著面具的傢伙，你認得嗎？」

「先生，他動作很快，而且又彎著腰，我真的沒看清楚。」是普爾的回答。「但如果你想問我，是不是海德先生？是的，我想是他沒錯。他們的身型差不多，矯健的動作也很類似，而且只有他能夠自由進出實驗室。先生你應該還記得，兇案發生

的時候鎖匙還留在兇手身上。但還有其他我說不上來的地方，厄特森先生，你見過海德嗎？」

「我跟他說過一次話。」律師回答

「那你一定也知道那位先生有點奇怪，十分不對勁，我也說不上來，就是給人一種冰冷刺骨的感覺。」

「我也有相同的感覺」厄特森先生說

「就是這樣，先生」普爾回答。「當那個戴著面具的東西，像猴子一樣從那堆化學品中跳起來跑回房間時，一股寒氣貫穿我的脊椎。厄特森先生，我看過一些書，知道這稱不上什麼證據。但這是我的直覺，我向上天發誓那就是海德先生。」

「好的，我想我們有同樣的擔憂，惡魔或許已經來了。我真心相信你說的話，我想可憐的亨利已經遇害了，而謀殺他的兇手還躲在他的房間裡（只有上帝才知道原因）。讓我們來為他復仇吧，你去把布萊蕭叫來。」

男僕聽令而來，面色發白又緊張。

「振作起來，布萊蕭。」律師說，「我知道大家都非常焦躁不安，我們現在就是要讓一切畫上句點。普爾跟我會破門而入，如果一切無礙，我會承擔所有責罵。但如果真的出了差錯，或是犯人要從後門逃跑，你和那個小夥子一定要帶著結實的棍子守住實驗室門口。我給你們十分鐘去守好出口。」

布萊蕭離開後，律師看了看他的手錶接著說，「普爾，我們現在開始行動吧。」他手上拿著火鉗進入院子。烏雲遮蔽了月亮，周遭陷入黑暗。風斷斷續續地吹進房子深處，蠟燭的光影在他們的腳下搖曳不定。兩人走到手術室前，坐下安靜地等待。整個倫敦在他們四周嗡嗡作響，但在近處，只有房間裡的踱步聲打破周遭的寧靜。

「先生，他每天都會像這樣踱步。」普爾悄聲說，「晚上也會走上很長的時間。只有藥局送藥來時，才會稍停一會兒。他必定是良心不安才會夜不成眠！先生，他的腳步聲沾滿了血跡啊！厄特森先生您靠近點，再仔細聽一次，這是不是醫生的腳步聲？」

那腳步聲輕盈又古怪，有一種奇異的節奏，非常緩慢，絕對和亨利傑寇爾沉重又嘎吱作響的步伐完全不同。厄特森先生嘆了一口氣，「沒有別的聲音了嗎？」他問。

普爾點了點頭說，「我有次曾聽到哭聲！」

「哭聲？真的嗎？」律師說，突然感到一陣戰慄。

管家說，「像女人或迷失的人會發出的哭聲。那聲音實在太哀傷，讓我聽到也難過得想哭。」

十分鐘過去了。普爾把斧頭從成堆的芒草下拿出，蠟燭放在桌上為接下來的攻擊做準備，他們屏住呼吸接近那在深夜仍舊來回不停踱步的腳步聲。

「傑寇爾，」厄特森高聲地說，「我一定要見你。」他停頓了一下，但沒有聽到回答。「這是善意的提醒，我們合理懷疑有不尋常的事發生了，所以我一定要見你一面。」他繼續說，「如果你不願意自行開門的話，我們只能強行進入了！」

「厄特森，看在老天的份上，可憐可憐我吧！

「這不是傑寇爾的聲音，這是海德！」厄特森大喊。「普爾，把門劈開！」

普爾高舉斧頭，用力向門板劈去。巨大的聲響讓整棟屋子都為之震動。那扇紅色絨布的門，像要掙脫門鎖和鉸鏈一樣跳了起來。門內傳出一聲像動物受驚的尖叫聲。斧頭繼續往下劈，門板和門框都碎裂了，普爾就這樣連砍了四次，但因為門的做工精良，一直到第五下時，堅固的門鎖才碎裂，厚實的門板終於往內倒在地毯上。

門外的兩人因為寂靜無聲的房間感到驚恐，紛紛往後退了一步，向裡頭望去。房裡點著燭光，壁爐裡燒著熊熊的爐火，水壺發出尖銳的聲音。一兩個抽屜開著，紙張在書桌上放得整整齊齊。爐火附近，擺放著茶具。除了滿滿的化學藥品外，這個安靜的房間跟倫敦其他地方一樣毫無異樣。

在房間中央躺著一個身體扭曲還在痛苦抽搐的男人。他們小心翼翼地靠近，把他翻過身，那是愛德華海德。他身上還穿著醫生的衣物，尺寸遠遠過大。他的臉還在顫抖著，但看得出來已經毫無生息。從他手中破碎的小藥瓶以及空氣中濃濃的杏仁味，厄特森知道這個男人自殺了。

「不管是要救他或是逮捕他，我們都來得太晚了。」他果斷地說。「海德已經死了，我們唯一能做的事就是找到你主人的屍體。」

　　整棟房子的一樓大部分都是手術室的空間，照明的光源在最上頭。房間位在樓上的一側，俯瞰庭院。手術室和一條走廊連結，可以通往小巷，而房間則有獨立的樓梯可進入。除此之外，還有一些黑暗的儲藏室跟一個寬敞的地下室。他們徹底地清查了這些地方。每個儲藏室只需要看一眼就夠了，因為它們全都空蕩蕩的。從門上飄落下來的灰塵可以知道，它們很久都沒開過了。地下室則擺滿了雜物，很多都是傑寇爾之前的屋主所遺留下來的物品。但當他們打開門時，飄下一片完美蜘蛛網顯示那個門也很久沒開過了，不需要進一步的搜索。到處都沒有亨利傑寇爾的蹤跡，不管他是死是活。

　　普爾踏著走廊的石板，聽著回聲說，「他一定被埋在這裡。」

　　「或者他逃走了。」厄特森邊說邊回頭檢視連接小巷的門。門鎖著，接著在石板的附近找到已然生鏽的鎖匙。

　　「這看起來很久沒用了，」律師觀察後說

　　「使用？」普爾接著說，「先生，您沒注意到它斷了嗎？像被人用腳狠狠踩過一樣。」

　　「的確，斷裂的地方也已經生鏽了。」兩個男人憂心忡忡地對望。「普爾，我不知道到底發生了什麼事，還是先回房間吧。」律師說。

他們倆沉默地踏上樓梯回到房間。恐懼地看了屍體一眼，然後開始更徹底地檢查房間裡的物品。一張桌子上有化學實驗的痕跡。一堆堆像是白色的鹽在玻璃淺碟上，就像有場實驗被不情願地打斷了。

「這就是我每次幫他買的藥，」普爾說。在這個時候水壺裡的水燒開了，發出了聲響。

他們循聲來到壁爐旁，一張安樂椅舒服地放在爐火旁，茶具也已經擺設完畢，杯子裡放了糖。架上有很多書，有本書攤開放在茶具旁。厄特森驚訝地發現那是一本神學著作，傑寇爾曾多次表達他對那本書的推崇，但現在卻看到他在上頭寫下的褻瀆批註。

他們繼續在房間的四周查看，然後走到穿衣鏡的前頭。兩人帶著恐懼的心情看向鏡子，卻只看到天花板上反射的光，壁爐裡折射了無數次的火光，還有櫥櫃的玻璃門，最後就是他們兩人蒼白又害怕的神情。

「先生，這個穿衣鏡一定見識到很多奇怪的事。」普爾悄聲說

「這面鏡子本身就很怪了。」律師同樣低聲地回答。「傑寇爾生前…」他嚇了一跳，連忙改口說，「傑寇爾拿這面鏡子做什麼呢？」他說

「你說的沒錯！」普爾回應

他們接著轉去查看辦公桌。桌上放著排列整齊的文件，其

中有個很大的信封，上頭有著醫生的字跡，寫著厄特森先生。律師打開那個信封，幾份文件掉到地上。第一份是遺囑，是傑寇爾醫生死亡或失蹤時的贈與契約，就跟他半年前退還的那份古怪遺囑一樣。但律師驚訝地發現上頭的受贈人名字不是愛德華海德，反而改成律師自己的名字了。他看了看普爾，然後又看了看文件，又望向躺在地上的犯人。

「我想不通到底發生了什麼事，」他說。「海德持有這份遺囑這麼多天，他不可能對我有任何好感，而且看到自己的名字被我取代一定非常憤怒，但他卻沒有毀了這份遺囑。」

他拿起下一張紙，那是醫生親筆寫的一張短箋，上頭註記著日期。律師驚呼著說，「喔，普爾！他今天還活著，他不可能在這麼短時間內就失蹤。他一定還活著，必定是逃走了！但為什麼要逃呢？又是怎麼逃的？那我們可以說海德是自殺的嗎？喔，我們必須小心謹慎，我不希望害你的主人陷入可怕的災難中。」

「先生，你何不打開那封信呢？」普爾問。

「因為我害怕，」律師憂心忡忡的回答，「上帝保佑我的憂慮不會成真！」話說完，他開始看短箋的內容。

「親愛的厄特森，等你收到這張便條時，我應該已經失蹤了。我無法預測我會怎麼失蹤，但我的直覺和無法言喻的情況告訴我，我的失蹤應該是注定會發生的事。請你去看藍恩給你的說明，他已經警告過我了。如果你還希望了解更多詳情，再看我的自白。」

「你不幸且配不上你的朋友」

「亨利傑寇爾」

「還有第三份文件？」厄特森問

「先生，在這。」普爾邊說邊遞給他一個密封嚴實的信封。

律師把文件放入口袋說，「關於這份文件，我不會多說什麼。如果你的主人逃走或死亡，我們至少可以保護他的名譽。已經十點了，我該回家安靜地讀這些文件了，但我午夜前可能會回來，到時候我們就可以報警了。」

他們走出去，把手術室的門鎖上。然後厄特森離開了在大廳聚集的僕人們，步行回辦公室，準備閱讀那兩份將解開所有謎團的文件。

Chapter

藍恩醫生記事

09

我如果不能徹底了解這團混亂，我就無法判斷它的重要性。

　　四天前，也就是一月九日，我在晚間收到一封掛號信。寄件者是同事和老同學，亨利傑寇爾。我非常驚訝收到他的信，因為我們從未有通信的習慣。我前晚才剛和他碰面，還一起吃了晚餐。我實在想不出任何要這麼正式的理由。信件的內容則讓我更加困惑，它的內容是這樣寫的：

　　12 月 10 日，18—

　　「親愛的藍恩－你是我認識最久的朋友之一，即便我們對科學的看法分歧，但我不認為我們的交情有因此受到影響，至少我單方面這麼覺得。如果哪天你跟我說，傑寇爾，我的生命、榮耀、理想都取決於你的決定，那麼即使要我砍掉左手，我也會義無反顧地幫你。藍恩，現在我的生命、榮耀、理想將任憑你處置了。我需要你為我做一件不光彩的事，請你做出決定。」

　　「我需要你延後今晚所有的安排，那怕是皇帝招喚你到他床前也一樣。坐上一台出租馬車，除非你自己的馬車正好停在門口。然後帶著這封信直接前往我家。我的管家普爾已經接到我的命令，會帶著一位鎖匠等你抵達。屆時請你們強行打開我的房門，然後你獨自進去。打開左手邊標著字母 E 的儲藏櫃，如果是鎖住的就直接打破它。把從上往下數的第四個抽屜或是由下往上數的第三個抽屜打開。因為我極度不安，所以非常害怕提供錯誤的資訊，但即便我的指令不正確，你還是可以依照抽屜裡的物品來推論是否打開正確的抽屜。裡頭應該有一些粉末，一個小玻璃瓶以及一本記事本。我懇求你把這個抽屜原封不動地帶回卡文迪什廣場。」

「這是第一部份的任務，現在是第二部份。如果你收到這封信之後立刻出發，你應該可以在午夜前回來，但我會預留一些時間。不僅是因為某些無法預防或預料的阻礙，也是因為當你的僕人入睡後，多出來的時間更適合進行剩下的事情。午夜時，我要你獨自待在診察室中，然後親自迎接一位我派去的男士，然後把抽屜交給他。到這裡，你的任務就完成了，也獲得我最高的感激之情。五分鐘後，如果你仍急切地需要完整的說明，你會明白這些安排有極為重要的意義，即便它們感覺起來非常奇異。如果其中任何一步有所閃失，你之後可能會為了我的死亡或是失去理智而受到良心的譴責。」

「即便我相信你不會拒絕我的請求，但一想到你可能會拒絕，我仍然十分害怕。請想像我此時此刻處在一個陌生的地方，深陷無法言喻的絕望黑暗之中。然而我清楚地知道，只要你能幫助我，我的困擾就能像個故事一樣順利完結。請你幫助我，親愛的藍恩，拯救我。」

你的朋友

亨利傑寇爾

「附註。一我把信密封後突然又感到一陣恐懼。郵局有可能無法準時寄送這封信，這樣一來你明早才會收到。如果是那樣的話，親愛的藍恩，請明天找方便的時間完成我的任務，我派去的信差應該還是會在午夜抵達。或許一切都已經太遲，如果當晚什麼事都沒發生的話，這就是亨利傑寇爾的最後遺言。」

看完這封信後，我確信我的同事已經失去理智了。但在能
證明這點前，我覺得有義務按照他的要求去做。我如果不能徹
底了解這團混亂，我就無法判斷它的重要性，用這種措辭寫
下的請求不能置之不理。於是我離開餐桌，搭上一台馬車前往
傑寇爾的住處。管家正在等我，他跟我一樣收到一封有著清楚
指示的掛號信，立刻派人去叫了鎖匠和木匠前來。我們還在交
談的時候這些工匠就到了，我們立刻前往老德曼醫生的手術
室，那裡是進入傑寇爾房間最快的地方（我相信你一定非常清
楚）。那扇門非常厚實，鎖也十分堅固。木匠說這件事有點棘
手，如果要強行進入的話他得把那扇門弄壞，而鎖匠則覺得無
能為力。幸好那位鎖匠手藝了得，經過兩小時的努力後，門終
於開了。我依照指示把標示 E 的櫃子打開，拿出那個抽屜，
用稻草塞滿，再用床單把抽屜包好，然後把它帶回卡文迪什廣
場。

之後，我檢查裡頭的內容物。那些粉末的包裝做工細緻，
但仍然不像專業藥劑師的成品，所以很明顯是傑寇爾自己做成
的。我打開包裝檢視，那些粉末看起來就像是晶瑩剔透的白色
結晶鹽。小玻璃瓶裡頭半滿，裝著血紅色的液體，味道聞起來
非常刺鼻，我認為應該有磷跟揮發性的乙醚，但其它的成份我
就一無所知了。記事本則毫無異樣，內容只有一系列的日期，
延續了好幾年，但我注意到大約一年前這些紀錄突然中斷了。
日期下還有一些零星的附註，通常不超過一個詞，例如「加倍」
這詞在數百條紀錄中大概出現過六次。在早期的紀錄裡，還曾
經出現過「徹底失敗！！！」這個附註，後頭還有三個驚嘆號。
這些資訊，雖然讓我大感好奇，但仍舊無法讓我理出頭緒。裝

著不知名液體的小玻璃瓶，一包成份不明的鹽，還有一系列沒有成果的實驗記錄（如同傑寇爾很多的研究一樣）。我家的這些物品為什麼會對我古怪同事的榮譽、理智或是生命有任何影響呢？如果他的信差能到這來，為什麼不能去別的地方呢？即便有些不便，為什麼要讓我秘密接待這位先生？我越想越覺得他一定是得了精神病，所以雖然我已經打發僕人去休息了，我還是把舊的左輪手槍上了膛，以防我有自衛的需要。

12 點的鐘響在倫敦響起，我聽到輕輕的敲門聲。開了門，我看到一個身材矮小的男人瑟縮在門廊的柱子旁。

「你是傑寇爾醫生派來的嗎？」我問

他姿勢彆扭地說「是的」。我請他入內後，他並未立即跟上，反而轉頭往漆黑的廣場探查。遠處有位警員拿著燈籠巡邏，一看到他，我的訪客猛然驚起，加快了腳步。

我承認這些細節讓我感到不甚愉快。我跟著他進入明亮的診療室時，手一直放在槍上。在這裡，我終於有機會看清楚他的臉。我從沒見過他，這點我很肯定。像我之前說的，他個頭很矮小。除了他臉上那讓人厭惡的神情，更讓我驚訝的是他雖然外表虛弱，但肌肉活動卻非常靈活。最後，就是他有一種異樣又讓人焦躁不安的感覺。這些都是初期僵硬和脈搏減弱的表徵。當時我認為這只是我個人主觀的厭惡之情，並對這些症狀的嚴重程度感到驚訝。但事後我相信這是人類的本能反應，比單純的喜惡之情更為直觀。

這個人（從他一進門我就感到一種令人不適的好奇心）的

穿著會讓正常人發笑。他身上的衣服雖然質料高級素雅，但尺寸實在太過寬大。褲子掛在腿上，得把褲管捲起來才不會拖地，外套的腰身已經蓋住臀部，領口敞開滑到肩膀上。奇怪的是，這樣滑稽的打扮並沒有讓我發笑。相反地，在我面前的這個生物，他本質中的異樣和不對勁，反而非常符合他的打扮，給人一種噁心又驚愕的感覺。因此，除了對這個人的本性和特質感到好奇外，我現在對於他的出身、生活、財富和在世界中扮演的角色也產生了好奇心。

這些觀察雖然看似相當透徹，但其實只花了幾秒鐘的時間。實際上，我的訪客已經等不及了。

「東西你拿到了嗎？」他大聲地說。「拿到了嗎？」他非常急切，甚至把手搭上了我的手臂，做似要搖晃我。

我把他的手推開，他的碰觸讓我打了一個寒顫。「先生，這邊請。你忘了你還沒自我介紹呢，請坐。」我說。我以身作則，先在習慣的位子上坐下，盡量仿效平常跟病人互動時的方式。但時間已經這麼晚了，加上我心中的眾多疑慮，還有對這個訪客的懼怕，我不知道表現得是否自然。

「藍恩醫生，不好意思。你說的很對，我過於急切都忘了禮貌。」他客氣地回答。「我受你同事亨利傑寇爾醫師所託，我了解…」他停了一下把手放在喉嚨上。我看得出來，即便他力圖鎮靜，他已經處在歇斯底里的邊緣了。「我知道，有個抽屜…」

或許是我對他感到同情，亦或是我實在太過好奇。

「先生，抽屜在那。」我說，指著桌子後方的地板，包著床單的抽屜就放在那。

他衝向它，然後停住，雙手摀著心口。我聽到他緊咬牙關，牙齒互磨的聲音，他的臉色變得非常不好，我開始擔心他的神智和生命。

「你冷靜一點。」我說

他轉頭望向我，露出一個可怕的笑容，然後像出於絕望一般，他一把拽下抽屜上的床單。看到裡頭的物品後，他發出了巨大的嗚咽聲，像是終於鬆了一口氣一樣，也把我嚇壞了。之後，他平復情緒，用平穩的音調問我，「你有刻度量杯嗎？」

我艱難地起身把量杯拿給他。

他微笑地向我點了點頭，倒出一些紅色液體，然後加入一些粉末。混合液一開始呈現紅色，但等到粉末開始融化，顏色就越變越淡，開始聽得到冒泡的聲音，也散發出少量的蒸氣。突然間沸騰停止，混合物變成深紫色，然後又再慢慢變成淡淡的綠色。我的訪客，一直保持著熱切地微笑，盯著這些變化。他把玻璃杯放在桌上，轉過身來，用審視的眼神看著我。

「現在，該進行接下來的步驟了」他說。「你會聰明地選擇嗎？你會遵守指令嗎？你會不需要我多做說明，就讓我把這個玻璃杯帶走嗎？還是你想滿足你的好奇心？回答之前請仔細考慮，因為你的決定會影響我的下一步。如果你什麼都不想知道，除了因為遵守承諾幫了我，而感到心安理得之外，你還是

會和原來一樣，不會比較富有也不會比較聰明。但若是你選擇
去理解一個全新領域的知識，你將因此獲得名望和權力。就在
此時此刻，在這個房間裡，你會大開眼界，目睹一個連惡魔都
無法置信的事。」

「先生，」我試著用毫不在意的口吻說，「你說的話讓人
費解。我想你應該明白我不是很相信你說的話吧。但我已經牽
涉太深，這件事必須要有個解釋才行。」

「那好吧，」我的訪客回答，「藍恩，你要記得曾許下的
醫生誓詞，接下來的事要嚴格保密。你們這些目光短淺，思想
狹隘，對超越傳統醫學推論總是嗤之以鼻的人老古板們，看好
了！」

他把玻璃杯拿到嘴邊，一口喝下。隨後他發出一聲尖叫，
身體搖晃踉蹌，抓住桌子穩住身體。他的眼睛瞪大，張著嘴巴
大口喘氣。我看著他，突然發現變化開始了。他整個人看來似
乎開始膨脹，臉色突然發黑，五官變得模糊，就像融化了一樣。
下個瞬間，我跳了起來背靠著牆壁，同時舉起手臂護住自己避
免受傷，我心中滿滿的都是恐懼。

「喔，天啊！」我尖叫出聲「喔，老天爺啊！」我不停地
叫。在我的眼前，出現了一個臉色蒼白，渾身顫抖，看似快要
暈過去的人。他像死而復生一樣，雙手胡亂揮舞，那是亨利傑
寇爾！

我無法寫下他在接下來那一小時中告訴我的事。我的所見
所聞讓我打從心底感到厭惡。現在，當那景象從我眼前徹底消

失後，我也無法確定這件事的真實性了。我的生命已被這事件徹底影響，我再也睡不著覺，而且時時刻刻都感到萬分恐懼。我感覺自己的日子所剩無多，即將死去，但我將帶著懷疑和困惑而死。至於那個男人向我展現的卑劣邪惡行徑，即使他曾流淚懺悔，我依然對此感到驚懼害怕，無法釋懷。厄特森，我只想說一件事（如果你相信我的話），根據傑寇爾的自白，那晚來我家的生物，叫做海德。全國各地都在追捕他，因為他就是殺害凱魯的兇手。

哈斯蒂藍恩

Chapter

亨利傑寇爾的自白

10

每個人，心中都同時有著善良和邪惡，
但是愛德華海德，他是人類中唯一的純粹邪惡個體。

　　我18— 年生於一個富裕的家庭，天資聰穎加上後天勤奮，獲得周遭智慧和良善人們的尊重。因此，一個光明和傑出的未來是必然的結果。但事實上，我也有個性上的缺點。和大眾無異，我喜歡追求歡愉的生活，但我的驕傲讓我不甘於和一般人一樣，所以總是以超乎想像的嚴肅面貌示人。因此我時常隱藏快樂，而當我開始反思己身之時，我檢視自己在這世界上所扮演的角色，我已經開始過著一種雙重生活。也許很多人會炫耀這種不符常規的行為，但因為我對自己有很高的標準，我以這些事情為恥，並設法隱藏它們。因此，與其說是我人格特質中的卑劣缺點讓我變成現在這樣，不如說是因為我與生俱來的偉大天性，讓善與惡的區別和界線，比大多數人更為深刻地在我的身上劃下了痕跡。

　　在這種情況之下，我不得不開始反思那些在生命中的嚴格定律，它是宗教信仰的根基，也是痛苦的來源。雖然我過著雙重生活，但我並不是偽君子。不管是在自我放縱陷入羞愧時，或在白天研究學問照看病患時，這兩種版本都是真實的我。而我超越常規的神祕學研究在這兩種意識彼此競爭之下，有了長足的進展。每一天，我體內中道德和智能的兩端讓我越來越靠近真相，而我也逐漸理解，人並非只有一面，而是兩面。我說兩面，是因為我自己的意識僅限於這兩種。未來其他人都將跟隨我的腳步，超越我的認知。我大膽地推測，最終人們會理解人都是擁有多種樣貌、矛盾卻又獨立的群體。至於我自己，出於我的本性，我僅會朝著一個方向前進。從自身和道德層面，我理解到人類原始的兩種面向。我看到這兩種意識在我體內相互抗衡，即便我能準確地說出我屬於哪一邊，那也是因為本質上的我兩者兼具。就算是在初期，當時我的科學研究尚未暗示這種奇蹟的可能時，我就已經時不時地沉醉在這種人格分離的白日夢當中。

我告訴我自己，如果兩種人格能擁有各自的身分，那麼生活將變得不再那麼難以忍受。邪惡的那方，可以不受道德理想的拘束，自由自在地過日子。正直的那方，也可以持續心安理得地去行善，而不會時刻被罪惡感所困擾。在痛苦的意識之中，這光譜兩端的特質持續地爭鬥，而這正是人類無法擺脫的矛盾宿命。那要怎麼做才能分離這兩方呢？

就在我陷入沉思的時候，有道側光照到實驗室的桌上。我開始更深入地思考，我們看似堅實的身體外殼，其實也跟薄霧一樣短暫，不是穩定的實體。我發現某種物質可以轉變我們的肉身，就像風能夠吹動窗簾一樣。我不會在這裡深入探討科學發現，是因為以下的兩個理由。首先，因為我已經明白，人類的肩上永遠擔負著生命的厄運和負擔，當我們想要卸下這個責任時，它們只會以更沉重和陌生的方式回到我們身上。其次，如同這份自白接下來的內容，我的科學發現並不完整。但我覺得已然足夠。我不僅從靈魂的光芒和氣息更為了解我的身體[1]，還成功配製出一種藥物，它能抑制我體內道德的力量，讓身體中第二種型貌取而代之。這過程對我來說同等自然，因

1　19世紀人們相信靈魂本質會影響人的外貌。內心邪惡的人外貌醜陋，心地善良的人則面貌姣好。

為它也是我的一部分，只是屬於較低階層的靈魂本質。

在實踐這個理論前我猶豫了很久，因為我深知這將帶來生命危險。任何能強大地控制和徹底改變身分的藥物，如果失手使用過量，或用在錯誤的時機點，都會毀了我的身體。但我實在無法抵抗能證明這獨特又深遠的科學發現機會。藥水我早就準備好了，並從一間批發藥商那購入了一大批特殊鹽類，我從之前的實驗得知，這是所需的最後成分。在一個該死的深夜，我把材料混合，看著它們在玻璃杯中沸騰冒煙。等到沸騰結束後，我鼓起勇氣，把藥水一口飲盡。

接著，我感到痛苦的折磨，骨頭劇烈摩擦、嚴重的噁心以及一種即便是生死存亡之際都無法感受到的恐懼。接著這些劇痛逐漸消失，我恢復意識，感覺好像大病初癒一樣。有什麼東西改變了，那是一種無法言喻的新奇感，甜美又異常。我覺得變得年輕，心中輕盈歡快，內心有種強烈的衝動輕率，一股像是水流一樣的混亂感受在我心中奔騰不息，解除了所有義務的束縛，是種未知但非良善的靈魂自由。從這個新生命的第一口呼吸開始，我就知道自己變邪惡了，十倍有餘的邪惡，我已屈服在我原始的邪惡本能之下。這個想法讓我感到溫暖而愉悅，就像品嘗了美酒一樣。我伸出雙手，陶醉在這種新鮮的感官體驗之中，而在這個當下，我突然意識到我的體型也改變了。

那時我的房間裡還沒有鏡子。現在我身旁的鏡子是之後才放進來的，目的正是為了這些變形。當時夜已深，即便四周黑暗也已快要接近破曉的時刻。我家中的同住者都還在沉睡之中，所以我在激動的心情之下決定要以這個新面貌進入臥房。

我穿過庭院，星星從頭頂上凝視著我。我想，它們必定也因為第一次看到這樣的生物而感到驚訝吧。我化身為一個陌生人，悄悄穿過走廊，進入我的房間，那是我第一次看到愛德華海德的模樣。

現在我只能針對理論進行論述，不是講我知道的，而是我認為最有可能的推論。我天性中的邪惡，也就是我現在已經具體呈現出來的部分，和良善的一面相比，更為弱小。因為在我的生命歷程中，我花費了九成的時間努力、做好事和自我控制，所以邪惡的部分相較之下，運用的時間額外的少，消耗的也少。所以愛德華海德才會比亨利傑寇爾來得矮小、纖細又較為年輕。當一個人的良善可以顯化在外表時，邪惡也能明顯地寫在另一個人的臉上。邪惡（我仍然相信它是人致命的一面）也在那個身體上留下了變形和衰敗的痕跡。但是當我看著鏡中那個醜陋的形貌時，我並未感到反感，反而產生一股歡迎之情。這個人也是我，同等自然又擁有人性。在我眼中，他展現出的靈魂生命力，比那不完美又矛盾分裂的我，更為直接純粹。在這方面我無疑是正確的。我發現當我以愛德華海德的形貌出現在大眾面前時，所有人在接近我的時候都展現出明顯的恐懼。我認為這是因為我們遇見的每個人，心中都同時有著善良和邪惡，但是愛德華海德，他是人類中唯一的純粹邪惡個體。

我並未在鏡子前逗留許久，因為我得進行第二次的實驗了。我現在還不知道是否能夠變身回第一個人格，如果已經無法恢復的話，我就得在天亮前逃出這個已經不再屬於我的房子。我快速地回到房間，準備好藥水喝下。再次承受肉體的折磨，然後變回我自己，成為亨利傑寇爾。

當晚，我迎來了命運的十字路口。如果這個實驗和科學發現是在崇高的理念或慷慨和虔誠的信仰下完成，一切都將有所不同。肉體上的痛苦，將會讓我成為天使而非惡魔。藥物沒有善惡之分，但它動搖了我囚禁在心中的劣根性，惡魔就像囚犯一樣逃脫了。那時我的美德在沉睡，我的邪惡則被野心喚醒，迅速機警地逮到機會，並以愛德華海德的面貌出現。因此我現在有兩種個性和外表，其中一個是全然的邪惡，另一個則是矛盾的混合體－亨利傑寇爾，對他我已經無心也無力來改造和改進了。因此這件事持續朝著最糟的方向發展下去。

即便在那個時候，我仍無法克服學術研究生活帶來的無趣。三不五時我還是希望能夠找點樂子，但因為我喜歡做的事並不那麼體面，加上我備受眾人的尊敬愛戴，而且逐漸步入老年，這種生活中的矛盾也漸漸帶來不便。因為如此，那種新力量的誘惑逐漸對我產生影響，接著我就再也無法自拔。我只要喝下藥水，就能去除這位知名教授的肉身，然後是穿上一襲厚重的外套，變身為愛德華海德。我喜歡這個念頭，在那時也仍舊認為是一件有趣的事。我為此非常細心地做了準備。我在蘇活區布置了房子，也就是警察追蹤到海德的那間房，另外又雇用了一位熟識的女僕當管家，她沉默寡言且道德低下。同時，我告訴我的僕人，有位海德先生（我描述了他的外貌），他能全權使用廣場的那間房屋。為了避免意外，我甚至親自以海德的身分出現，讓他們熟悉這個人。接下來我起草了那份你非常反感的遺囑。要是傑寇爾醫生這個身分發生任何意外，愛德華海德就可以直接接收他名下的所有財產。我認為這樣的安排萬無一失，所以開始享受這種奇異身分所帶來的特權。

以前有人會為了保護自己的身份地位，雇用亡命之徒犯罪。而我是第一個為了享樂而這樣做的人。前一秒我還是一位眾人愛戴，身份尊貴的醫生，但下個瞬間，我就能像個脫下制服的學生一樣，過著隨心所欲自由自在的生活。對我來說，穿在身上的是一件無堅不摧的斗篷，我的安全無懈可擊。想像一下，我根本不存在！只要我進入實驗室，花幾秒鐘混合備好的材料，在喝下藥水後，不管愛德華海德做了什麼，他就像是一股呼在鏡子上的氣息，即刻消失無蹤。而安靜待在書房裡修剪燭芯的亨利傑寇爾，對任何懷疑都站得住腳。

如我先前所說，我那些急於在偽裝之下獲得的樂趣並不體面，我甚至不敢說得更為直白。但在愛德華海德的身份下，那些樂趣很快地變得駭人且怪異。當我從那些遠行歸來時，我對在化身時所犯下的墮落罪行感到困惑。屬於我靈魂中的邪惡，獨自出發尋歡，他的每個舉動和想法都以自我為中心，擁有像野獸一樣的貪慾，樂於折磨他人，以他們的苦難為樂，冰冷無情。亨利傑寇爾時常對愛德華海德的惡行感到驚訝，但這情況有違常理，所以暗中地放下了良心的譴責。畢竟這是海德獨自一人的作為，有罪的是海德，傑寇爾和此事無關。甦醒後他的良善沒有任何損傷，他甚至會儘快地修正海德所犯下的壞事，所以他的良心也就不會過意不去了。

我無意深入討論我的惡行細節（即使到了現在我仍然不敢

承認我犯了罪），我只是想點出給我的警告和懲罰已慢慢顯現。我發生了一個意外，因為後果並不嚴重，我只會簡單帶過。有個路人因為我對一個孩童做的殘忍行為忿忿不平，之後我才知道他是你的親戚。小孩的家人和醫生也和他一樣非常憤怒，我當時有些擔心我的生命安全，最後，為了平息他們的怒火，愛德華海德不得不帶他們回家，並給他們一張亨利傑寇爾開出的支票。之後，我在其他銀行用愛德華海德的名字開了一個戶頭，就把這個問題輕鬆地解決了。我用不同的角度簽下愛德華海德名字，當時，我以為我已經逃離了命運的箝制。

約在丹佛爵士遇害的兩個月前，我從一場遠行歸來，到家時已然深夜。第二天醒來時，我感到有些異常。我茫然地四處張望，我的確是在廣場的房間裡沒錯。寬大的空間、高級的家具、床帷的樣式還有桃花心木的床框都是我熟悉的樣子。但是不知道為什麼，我總感覺我其實是在蘇活區的小房間裡，在那個愛德華海德休息的地方。我笑自己太傻，然後用心理分析的方式探究這種錯覺的成因，接著不知不覺又開始打盹。半夢半醒的瞬間，我看到了我的手。亨利傑寇爾的手又大又結實，皮膚白皙形狀優美（你之前也曾這樣說過）。但倫敦上午日光下的這隻手，卻是瘦骨嶙峋，顏色黯淡，還長著濃密的毛髮。這是愛德華海德的手。

我動也不動地盯著它，停了近半分鐘之久，陷入全然地迷惑中。爾後心中湧起的恐懼，像一聲巨響，讓我從床上彈了起來。我匆忙衝向鏡子，眼前看到的景象讓我的血液幾乎凍結。我入睡時是亨利傑寇爾，但醒來時卻變成了愛德華海德。我問我自己，為什麼會這樣呢？然後恐懼再次湧上心頭，我該如何解決這個問題？現在已經是早上了，僕人們也都已經起床，我所有的藥劑都在另一個房間裡，要走下兩層樓梯，穿過後門的通道，再經過露天庭院和解剖學教室，想到這裡我就嚇得無法動彈。或許我有辦法遮住我的臉，但那又有什麼用呢，因為身材的變化是沒法遮掩的。後來，我想到僕人們其實已經習慣了我的化身在這裡來來去去，所以也就不再焦慮。我快速地穿上符合我現在尺寸的衣服，很快地穿過房子。布萊蕭一早看到海德先生這樣奇怪的行徑就退了回去。十分鐘後，傑寇爾醫生恢復了原本的樣貌，心不在焉地坐下吃著早餐。

　　這無從解釋的事件，和我之前的經驗完全相反，就像個凶兆，正寫下對我的判決。我也因此用更嚴肅的態度，思考這第二身分將帶來的問題和可能性。我投射出的那個人格，現在更頻繁地出現和接受滋養，愛德華海德的身體最近似乎變高了。我成為他的時候，能感到體內的血液更強烈地流動，如果這種狀況持續下去，這兩種人格的平衡可能會瓦解，讓我以後再也無法自由變身，而愛德華海德將成為唯一的我。藥物並非萬靈丹。在我剛當上醫生時，曾碰過藥物完全失靈的狀況。之後，也曾碰過需要加倍劑量的時刻。甚至還有一次，得冒著生命危險，把劑量調高到三倍之多。我的現況在這種不確定的因素之下有了一絲陰影。那天早上的事件讓我留意到，現在變身時的困難，已經從難以擺脫傑寇爾的身體，到無法掙脫海德的掌控了。這所有的線索似乎都指向同一點，那就是我開始慢慢喪失對自己的控制，並且緩慢地成為第二個人格，也就是較糟糕的那一個。

我必須在這兩者間做出選擇。這兩個人格雖有共同的記憶，但其他方面差異很大。傑寇爾有敏銳的理解力，也樂於參與海德的冒險，分享他的樂趣。但海德對傑寇爾卻漠不關心，亦或只把他當作藏身躲避的洞穴。傑寇爾就像是父親，海德則是冷漠的兒子。如果選擇了傑寇爾，就代表我得放棄以來一直隱藏的慾望還有近期的放縱享樂。若選擇海德，我則必須放棄以往的喜好和抱負，並永遠變成一個讓人輕視，沒有朋友的傢伙。這場交易看來不太公平，但我還有其他需要考量的地方。選擇傑寇爾，我將因為自我克制而備受折磨，但海德卻不會意識到失去的東西。雖然我的處境特殊，但這和一般人的日常生活無異，我們要抵抗誘惑做出決定。和大多數人一樣，我選了更好的那一面，但卻無法堅持下去。

沒錯，我更喜歡那位年邁不滿的醫生，他有朋友也有正直的慾望。我堅定地告別了海德帶來的自由輕快，慾望衝動和隱藏的樂趣。也許在潛意識之下，我仍有所保留，因為我既沒有放棄蘇活區的房子，也仍然把愛德華海德的衣物整齊地放在櫥櫃裡。兩個月來，我過著比以前都更為嚴謹的日子，心安理得。但時間最終磨損了我的警戒，心安理得的日子變得理所當然，我開始受到苦悶和慾望的折磨，就像海德在追求自由一樣。最後在一個軟弱的時刻，我再次喝下了變身藥水。

我想每個酒鬼都不會在乎酗酒對他造成的影響，就像我也從未真切地體認到愛德華海德的危險。他對道德和惡行的全然麻木是我遭受懲罰的主因。我的惡魔因為被囚禁了太久，怒吼著掙脫牢籠，我在一喝下藥劑時就即刻感受到一股更為放縱和狂暴的邪惡意圖。我猜想，正是這種在靈魂深處攪動的不耐情緒，才會讓我在被害人禮貌的詢問前徹底失控。我向上帝發誓，沒有一個正常人會在這種狀況下犯下如此罪行。就像是一個生病的小孩打破玩具一樣，這是唯一合理的解釋。即便是最糟糕的人，在誘惑之前也能以某種程度找到平衡繼續前進，但是我自甘墮落放棄控制。所以對我來說，即便是最輕微的誘惑，也讓我徹底墜落。

從地獄而來的靈魂立即甦醒。我在狂喜的狀態下折磨著無力反抗的身體，每一次的重擊都讓我感到滿心雀躍，直到疲勞感襲來，我才在狂暴的巔峰中突然感到一陣刺骨的恐懼穿過心臟。迷霧散去，我覺得我的人生完了。我抱著得意又激動的心情從犯罪現場逃走。邪惡的慾望被滿足了，此時我的求生本能凌駕了一切。我跑到蘇活區的房子，確認所有海德的文件都已經銷毀，接著穿過昏暗的小巷，還對犯下的罪行沾沾自喜，輕挑地想著未來的邪惡計畫。同時間加快腳步，留意著後面的追緝者。海德輕快地哼著曲子調配藥劑，他在喝下藥水時向死者致敬。變身的痛苦還沒未消退前，亨利傑寇爾已經淚流滿面，悔恨地跪倒在地，舉起雙手向上帝禱告。自我放逐的面紗已被完全撕裂。我的一生在我眼前展現，從幼時牽著父親的手，到職業生涯中的自我砥礪，一遍又一遍，那晚發生的事仍舊令人無法置信又萬分驚悚。我差點尖叫出聲，試圖用眼淚和祈禱抑制在腦海中出現的醜陋影像和聲音。然而在祈禱之間，我那張邪惡的面孔依舊緊盯著我。隨著悔恨迅速退去，我的心頭湧上一陣喜悅。我已經把問題解決了，海德再也無法出現。喔，一想到這點我就非常高興。我願意抱著謙卑的心，過著自我克制的新人生。因為我已心甘情願地鎖住那扇時常進出的門，還把鑰匙也毀了。

第二天，謀殺案的消息傳了開來。海德殺害了一位備受公眾愛戴的人，全世界的人都知道他犯下的罪行。這不只是一起案件，更是一個悲劇的愚蠢行為。我想我為此感到慶幸，因為我的衝動將被恐懼抑制。傑寇爾是我的避風港，要是海德稍微洩露蹤跡，所有的人都會群起殺之。

我下定決心要用未來的行為替過去贖罪。我可以真切地說，我做了很多善事。你也知道，去年底我替別人操持了很多事，日子過得十分平靜，我幾乎感到快樂。我並不厭倦這種行善和純真的生活，相反地，我越來越享受每一天。但我依舊受到雙重人格的詛咒，當懺悔之情逐漸減弱時，我那被遏止又長期放縱的卑劣性格，又開始咆哮著想要自由。並非是我希望再度喚醒海德，一想到他就讓我發狂。這種慾望源自我的根本，挑戰我的良心。最後我就像個秘密的罪人一樣，再度被誘惑攻擊而跌下深淵。

一切都將畫上句點，我已經抵達我的極限。這次我對邪惡的忽視，終究摧毀了靈魂的平衡。但我並未察覺危險即將襲來，這次的崩毀來得那麼自然。我就像回到了從前的日子一樣。那是個美好又晴朗的一月天，霜在腳下融化，天空萬里無雲，倫敦的攝政公園充斥著冬天的鳥鳴還有春天的芬芳氣味。我坐在長椅上曬著太陽，體內的獸性蠢蠢欲動，靈魂仍似睡非

睡，想著要繼續懺悔贖罪，但還未開始進行。我想著，終究我
也和一般人沒有兩樣。然後我笑了出來，我怎會把自己和其他
人相比，我積極地做了這麼多善事，別人可是冷漠懶散又殘
忍。就在這個自滿的瞬間，一陣猛烈的噁心不適襲來，我感到
一股致命的戰慄。這些感覺消失後我昏了過去。待我甦醒後，
我發覺我的想法有了變化，我變得更加莽撞衝動，對於危險不
屑一顧，不再受到義務的約束。我低頭一看，衣服鬆垮地掛在
我縮小的四肢上，放在膝蓋上的手，骨節明顯，有著濃密的毛
髮。我又變為愛德華海德了。前一刻我還非常富有，而且備受
眾人愛戴尊敬，家裡的餐廳已經準備完畢，等著我回去用餐。
但現在，我卻成為大家都知道的兇手，是所有人追捕的對象，
無家可歸，屬於絞刑架上的死囚。

　　我的狀況雖然不太穩定，但尚未完全失去理智。經我多次
觀察發現，在第二人格中，我的其他感官變得更為靈敏緊繃，
但也富有彈性。所以當發生了傑寇爾無法應付的事件時，海
德就會取而代之。我的藥物都鎖在房間的衣櫃裡，我該怎麼辦
呢？我用手按著太陽穴想著該如何解決這個問題。我已經關上
了實驗室的門，如果要從房子裡進入，我的僕人肯定會報警把
我抓起來。我必定得找其他人幫忙，於是我想到了藍恩。我該
怎麼跟他聯繫？又能如何說服他？假設我能在街頭逃過追捕，
我又該如何和他碰面呢？我這個不受歡迎的陌生訪客，該怎樣
才能說服這位知名的醫生，前往搜查他同事傑寇爾的書房？接
著，我想起我仍保有原來身份的某部分，那就是我的筆跡。我

一想到這個絕妙的點子，一切都豁然開朗。

　　接著，我盡力讓衣服合身，雇了一台路過的馬車，前往波特蘭街的一間旅社，我碰巧還記得它的名字。一看到我的穿著，車夫無法掩飾他的笑意（雖然這衣物之下的身體有著悲劇的命運，但實際上真的十分滑稽）。我咬牙切齒地瞪著他，散發出魔鬼才會有的怒意，讓他的笑臉頓時消失無蹤。這對我倆都是好事，不然我絕對會把他從座位上扯下來。進入旅社後，我臉上的陰沉神色，讓旅社員工都萬分恐懼。接待我的時候，他們一句話都不敢多說，只恭敬地接收指令。之後他們給了我一間單人房，並提供需要的東西讓我寫信。生命受到威脅的海德是一種全新的體驗，他體內有著無法抑制的憤怒，瀕臨殺人的邊緣，渴望對人造成傷害。但這個生物非常精明，他用強大的意志力控制住怒氣，寫好了兩封信，一封給藍恩，一封給普爾。為了確保這兩封信被順利寄出，他要求用掛號方式寄送。接下來的一整天，他都坐在房間的壁爐旁，咬著指甲。他在房間裡獨自進食，和恐懼共處，服務人員明顯地都很怕他。等到夜晚終於降臨時，他招來一輛馬車，在城市的街頭來回遊蕩。他，或是我…也不能說是我。這個惡魔的化身毫無人性，體內除了恐懼和仇恨，別無他物。在馬車駕駛起了疑心之後，他就下了馬車改為步行。身上明顯不合身的衣物，讓他格外引人注目。他走進深夜的人群中，恐懼和仇恨在心中碰撞發酵。他走得很快，被恐懼追趕，自言自語，專挑人煙稀少的小巷行走，計算著離午夜時分還有多久。後來有個女人跟他搭話，也許是想兜售火柴。他打了她一巴掌，她逃走了。

　　當我在藍恩家恢復意識時，那位老友對我的恐懼或許影響了我，我沒辦法確定。畢竟，和那段時間經歷的厭惡和憎恨相比，那點恐懼實在算不了什麼。我的想法改變了，我害怕的不再是上絞刑台，而是懼怕再度成為海德。我恍惚地接受藍恩的責罵，也是在意識模糊的狀態之下回到家，上床休息。經過筋疲力竭的一天後，我陷入深沉的睡眠，就算是做了噩夢也無法讓我驚醒。我在早晨醒來，感到虛弱不堪，但精神抖擻。我依舊害怕那寄居在我身體裡的惡魔，對前一天令人膽戰心驚的危險也歷歷在目。但我已經安全地回家了，在我自己的房間裡，隨時都有藥可用。逃過一劫的心情是如此激動，讓我感到未來光明可期。

　　早餐之後，正當我悠閒地在庭院漫步，享受早晨的寒冷空氣時，我再次被那難以形容的感覺襲擊，這正是變身的前兆。我的時間只夠我躲進房間，然後我就再度被海德所支配。這次，我需要兩倍的藥劑才有辦法變回原來的自己，而且！這次的效果竟然只維持了六個小時。當我神色哀戚地坐在爐火旁，那劇痛又再次襲來，我得再度服藥。簡而言之，從那天起，我得非常努力，並且依靠藥物的控制，才有辦法維持傑寇爾的身份。無論是白天或晚上，我都會感到變身前的顫抖。特別是在我入睡後，又或是在椅子上打盹兒休息時，我總會以海德的樣貌醒來。死亡末日所帶來的巨大壓力，加上我強迫自己減少睡眠時間，已經到了人體無法承受的地步，我原來的身體開始高燒不退，健康急速下滑，身體和心靈都越來越衰弱，直到腦海完全被一個念頭佔據，那就是對另一個自己的恐懼。當我睡著，或是藥物的功效消退時，我幾乎已經可以跳過變身的過程

（痛苦的程度也越來越低），直接變成海德，腦海中充斥著恐怖的畫面，心中懷抱著無緣由的憎恨，身體似乎已經無法承載洶湧的生命能量。

海德的力量隨著傑寇爾的日漸衰弱似乎變得更為強大。現在他們彼此憎恨。對傑寇爾來說，那是一種生命本能。最讓他感到痛苦的部分是，他必須和海德分享意識共享死亡。但除此之外，海德這個惡魔，雖然有著豐沛的生命力，也就只是一個非人的存在。這就像是爛泥竟然能張口喊叫出聲，看不見的塵埃有能力犯下滔天大罪一樣，沒有形體的死物竟然有奪取生命的能力，這是多麼不可思議啊！和我緊密連結又無法分割的恐怖羈絆，被囚禁在我的肉體之中，我可以聽到它的低語和奮力掙扎。在每個軟弱或是沉睡的時刻，它就會破繭而出，奪取我的身體。

但海德對傑寇爾的憎恨則有所不同。因為害怕被送上絞刑台，他一直委曲求全，不斷退回第二人格的位置。但他痛恨這樣，也討厭傑寇爾的沮喪心情，更無法忍受他人對他的嫌惡。因此，他會使出一些低階的把戲來報復我，像在我的書頁上寫上一些褻瀆上帝的字眼，燒毀我的信件，破壞我父親的畫像。要不是因為他恐懼死亡，他一定會跟我同歸於盡的。但他對生命的熱愛令人驚奇。雖然一想到他，我就感覺噁心害怕，但每次我一察覺到他有多麼害怕我會自殺，讓他一同死去，我竟對他產生了憐憫之情。

多說無益，時間已經迫在眉梢。沒人受過這種折磨，這樣就夠了，而即便我已逐漸習慣這些折磨，並不是因為狀況有所緩解，而是因為我的靈魂已經感到麻不，也已經逐漸接受絕望。這種懲罰本可以持續多年，但最後的一根稻草已經落下，終於讓我和自己的本性分道揚鑣。從第一次實驗後，我尚未重新購買過鹽類，現在已經快要用完了。我派人再度前往購買，調製了藥水。和之前一樣，藥水開始沸騰，卻只出現了第一次的變色，第二次的變色消失無蹤。我把藥水喝了下去，但沒有效果。你應該已經聽普爾說了，為了購買鹽類我翻遍了整個倫敦，但一切的努力都只是徒勞無功。我現在認為是購買的第一批的貨品成分不純，正是其中的混雜物才讓藥劑有了功效。

　　一週過去了，這份陳述是我在最後一批舊粉末的藥效下寫的。這也是最後一次，亨利傑寇爾能自主思考並看到鏡中的自己（很不幸地，這張臉已經變了！）。我得非常小心再加上萬分幸運才能順利把信寫完。如果寫到中途，我又開始變身，海德就會把它撕成碎片。但如果寫完後我還有多一點時間，那麼依照海德只在乎當下和自私的性格，或許這封信就能順利保存下來。的確，他已經被即將降臨到我倆身上的厄運壓垮了。半小時後，當我永遠變成那個可恨的人時，我會否坐在椅子上顫抖哭泣，亦或是焦急地聽著外頭的聲音，揣測每一個可能的威脅，持續在房內來回踱步（這是我在這世間最後一個避難所）。海德會在絞刑台上死去嗎？或是他會在最後一刻鼓起勇氣結束自己的生命？只有老天才知道，而我一點都不在乎。現在就是我死亡的時刻，接下來的事都和我再無關係。我在此停筆，密封這份自白，結束痛苦的亨利傑寇爾的生命。

Chapter

Story of the Door

01

You start a question, and it's like starting a stone.
You sit quietly on the top of a hill;
and away the stone goes, starting others.

Mr. Utterson the lawyer was a man of a rugged countenance that was never lighted by a smile; cold, scanty and embarrassed in discourse; backward in sentiment; lean, long, dusty, dreary and yet somehow lovable. At friendly meetings, and when the wine was to his taste, something eminently human beaconed from his eye; something indeed which never found its way into his talk, but which spoke not only in these silent symbols of the after-dinner face, but more often and loudly in the acts of his life. He was austere with himself; drank gin when he was alone, to mortify a taste for vintages; and though he enjoyed the theatre, had not crossed the doors of one for twenty years. But he had an approved tolerance for others; sometimes wondering, almost with envy, at the high pressure of spirits involved in their misdeeds; and in any extremity inclined to help rather than to reprove. "I incline to Cain's heresy," he used to say quaintly: "I let my brother go to the devil in his own way." In this character, it was frequently his fortune to be the last reputable acquaintance and the last good influence in the lives of down-going men. And to such as these, so long as they came about his chambers, he never marked a shade of change in his demeanour.

No doubt the feat was easy to Mr. Utterson; for he was undemonstrative at the best, and even his friendship seemed to be founded in a similar catholicity of good-nature. It is the mark of a modest man to accept his friendly circle ready-made from the hands of opportunity; and that was the lawyer's way. His friends were those of his own blood or those whom he had known the longest; his affections, like ivy, were the growth of time, they implied no aptness in the object. Hence, no doubt the bond that united him to Mr. Richard Enfield, his distant kinsman, the well-known man about town. It was a nut to crack for many, what these two could see in each other, or what subject they could find in common. It was reported by those who encountered them in their Sunday walks, that they said nothing, looked singularly dull and would hail with obvious relief the appearance of a friend. For all that, the two men put the greatest store by these excursions, counted them the chief jewel of each week, and not only set aside occasions of pleasure, but even resisted the calls of business, that they might enjoy them uninterrupted.

It chanced on one of these rambles that their way led them down a by-street in a busy quarter of London. The street was small and what is called quiet, but it drove a thriving trade on the weekdays. The inhabitants were all doing well, it seemed and all emulously hoping to do better still, and laying out the surplus of their grains in coquetry; so that the shop fronts stood along that thoroughfare with an air of invitation, like rows of smiling saleswomen. Even on Sunday, when it veiled its more florid charms and lay comparatively empty of passage, the street shone out in contrast to its dingy neighbourhood, like a fire in a forest; and with its freshly painted shutters, well-polished brasses, and general cleanliness and gaiety of note, instantly caught and pleased the eye of the passenger.

Two doors from one corner, on the left hand going east, the line was broken by the entry of a court; and just at that point, a certain sinister block of building thrust forward its gable on the street. It was two storeys high; showed no window, nothing but a door on the lower storey and a blind forehead of discoloured wall on the upper; and bore in every feature, the marks of prolonged and sordid negligence. The door, which was equipped with neither bell nor knocker, was blistered and distained. Tramps slouched into the recess and struck matches on the panels; children kept shop upon the steps; the schoolboy had tried his knife on the mouldings; and for close on a generation, no one had appeared to drive away these random visitors or to repair their ravages.

Mr. Enfield and the lawyer were on the other side of the by-street; but when they came abreast of the entry, the former lifted up his cane and pointed.

"Did you ever remark that door?" he asked; and when his

companion had replied in the affirmative, "It is connected in my mind," added he, "with a very odd story."

"Indeed?" said Mr. Utterson, with a slight change of voice, "and what was that?"

"Well, it was this way," returned Mr. Enfield: "I was coming home from some place at the end of the world, about three o'clock of a black winter morning, and my way lay through a part of town where there was literally nothing to be seen but lamps. Street after street and all the folks asleep—street after street, all lighted up as if for a procession and all as empty as a church—till at last I got into that state of mind when a man listens and listens and begins to long for the sight of a police-man. All at once, I saw two figures: one a little man who was stumping along eastward at a good walk, and the other a girl of maybe eight or ten who was running as hard as she was able down a cross street. Well, sir, the two ran into one anoth-er naturally enough at the corner; and then came the horrible part of the thing; for the man trampled calmly over the child's body and left her screaming on the ground. It sounds noth-ing to hear, but it was hellish to see. It wasn't like a man; it was like some damned Juggernaut. I gave a few halloa, took to my heels, collared my gentleman, and brought him back to where there was already quite a group about the screaming child. He was perfectly cool and made no resistance, but gave me one look, so ugly that it brought out the sweat on me like running. The people who had turned out were the girl's own family; and pretty soon, the doctor, for whom she had been sent put in his appearance. Well, the child was not much the worse, more frightened, according to the sawbones; and there you might have supposed would be an end to it. But there was one curious circumstance. I had taken a loathing to my gentleman at first sight. So had the child's family, which was only natural. But the doctor's case was what struck me. He was the usual cut and dry apothecary, of no particular age and colour, with a strong Edinburgh accent and about as emotional as a bagpipe. Well, sir, he was like the rest of us; every time he looked at my prisoner, I saw that sawbones turn sick and white with the desire to kill him. I knew what was in his mind, just as he knew what was in mine; and killing being out of the question, we did the next best. We told the man we could and would make such a scandal out of this as should make his name stink from one end of London to the other. If he had any friends or any credit, we undertook that he should lose them. And all the time, as we were pitching it in red hot, we were keeping the women off him as best we could for they were as wild as harpies. I never saw a circle of such hateful faces; and there was the man in the middle, with a kind of black sneering coolness—frightened too, I could see that—

but carrying it off, sir, really like Satan. 'If you choose to make capital out of this accident,' said he, 'I am naturally helpless. No gentleman but wishes to avoid a scene,' says he. 'Name your figure.' Well, we screwed him up to a hundred pounds for the child's family; he would have clearly liked to stick out; but there was something about the lot of us that meant mischief, and at last he struck. The next thing was to get the money; and where do you think he carried us but to that place with the door?—whipped out a key, went in, and presently came back with the matter of ten pounds in gold and a cheque for the balance on Coutts's, drawn payable to bearer and signed with a name that I can't mention, though it's one of the points of my story, but it was a name at least very well known and often printed. The figure was stiff; but the signature was good for more than that, if it was only genuine. I took the liberty of pointing out to my gentleman that the whole business looked apocryphal, and that a man does not, in real life, walk into a cellar door at four in the morning and come out with another man's cheque for close upon a hundred pounds. But he was quite easy and sneering. 'Set your mind at rest,' says he, 'I will stay with you till the banks open and cash the cheque my-self.' So we all set off, the doctor, and the child's father, and our friend and myself, and passed the rest of the night in my chambers; and next day, when we had breakfasted, went in a body to the bank. I gave in the cheque myself, and said I had every reason to believe it was a forgery. Not a bit of it. The cheque was genuine."

"Tut-tut!" said Mr. Utterson.

"I see you feel as I do," said Mr. Enfield. "Yes, it's a bad story. For my man was a fellow that nobody could have to do with, a really damnable man; and the person that drew the cheque is the very pink of the proprieties, celebrated too, and (what makes it worse) one of your fellows who do what they call good. Blackmail, I suppose; an honest man paying through the nose for some of the capers of his youth. Black Mail House is what I call the place with the door, in consequence. Though even that, you know, is far from explaining all," he added, and with the words fell into a vein of musing.

From this he was recalled by Mr. Utterson asking rather suddenly: "And you don't know if the drawer of the cheque lives there?"

"A likely place, isn't it?" returned Mr. Enfield. "But I happen to have noticed his address; he lives in some square or other."

"And you never asked about the—place with the door?" said Mr. Utterson.

"No, sir; I had a delicacy," was the reply. "I feel very strongly about putting questions; it partakes too much of the style of the day of judgment. You start a question, and it's like starting a stone. You sit quietly on the top of a hill; and away the stone goes, starting others; and presently some bland old bird (the last you would have thought of) is knocked on the head in his own back garden and the family have to change their name. No sir, I make it a rule of mine: the more it looks like Queer Street, the less I ask."

"A very good rule, too," said the lawyer.

"But I have studied the place for myself," continued Mr. Enfield. "It seems scarcely a house. There is no other door, and nobody goes in or out of that one but, once in a great while, the gentleman of my adventure. There are three windows looking on the court on the first floor; none below; the windows are always shut but they're clean. And then there is a chimney which is generally smoking; so somebody must live there. And yet it's not so sure; for the buildings are so packed together about the court, that it's hard to say where one ends and another begins."

The pair walked on again for a while in silence; and then

"Enfield," said Mr. Utterson, "that's a good rule of yours."

"Yes, I think it is," returned Enfield.

"But for all that," continued the lawyer, "there's one point I want to ask. I want to ask the name of that man who walked over the child."

"Well," said Mr. Enfield, "I can't see what harm it would do. It was a man of the name of Hyde."

"Hm," said Mr. Utterson. "What sort of a man is he to see?"

"He is not easy to describe. There is something wrong with his appearance; something displeasing, something down-right detestable. I never saw a man I so disliked, and yet I scarce know why. He must be deformed somewhere; he gives a strong feeling of deformity, although I couldn't specify the point. He's an extraordinary looking man, and yet I really can name nothing out of the way. No, sir; I can make no hand of it; I can't describe him. And it's not want of memory; for I declare I can see him this moment."

Mr. Utterson again walked some way in silence and obviously under a weight of consideration. "You are sure he used a key?" he inquired at last.

"My dear sir..." began Enfield, surprised out of himself.

"Yes, I know," said Utterson; "I know it must seem strange. The fact is, if I do not ask you the name of the other party, it is because I know it already. You see, Richard, your tale has gone home. If you have been inexact in any point you had better correct it."

"I think you might have warned me," returned the other with a touch of sullenness. "But I have been pedantically exact, as you call it. The fellow had a key; and what's more, he has it still. I saw him use it not a week ago."

Mr. Utterson sighed deeply but said never a word; and the young man presently resumed. "Here is another lesson to say nothing," said he. "I am ashamed of my long tongue. Let us make a bargain never to refer to this again."

"With all my heart," said the lawyer. "I shake hands on that, Richard."

Chapter

Search for Mr. Hyde

02

O my poor old Harry Jekyll,
if ever I read Satan's signature upon a face,
it is on that of your new friend.

That evening Mr. Utterson came home to his bachelor house in sombre spirits and sat down to dinner without relish. It was his custom of a Sunday, when this meal was over, to sit close by the fire, a volume of some dry divinity on his reading desk, until the clock of the neighbouring church rang out the hour of twelve, when he would go soberly and gratefully to bed. On this night, however, as soon as the cloth was taken away, he took up a candle and went into his business room. There he opened his safe, took from the most private part of it a document endorsed on the envelope as Dr. Jekyll's Will and sat down with a clouded brow to study its contents. The will was holograph, for Mr. Utterson, though he took charge of it now that it was made, had refused to lend the least assistance in the making of it; it provided not only that, in case of the decease of Henry Jekyll, M.D., D.C.L., L.L.D., F.R.S., etc., all his possessions were to pass into the hands of his "friend and benefactor Edward Hyde," but that in case of Dr. Jekyll's "disappearance or unexplained absence for any period exceeding three calendar months," the said Edward Hyde should step into the said Henry Jekyll's shoes without further delay and free from any burthen or obligation beyond the payment of a few small sums to the members of the doctor's household. This document had long been the lawyer's eyesore. It offended him both as a lawyer and as a lover of the sane and customary sides of life, to whom the fanciful was the immodest. And hitherto it was his ignorance of Mr. Hyde that had swelled his indignation; now, by a sudden turn, it was his knowledge. It was already bad enough when the name was but a name of which he could learn no more. It was worse when it began to be clothed upon with detestable attributes; and out of the shifting, insubstantial mists that had so long baffled his eye, there leaped up the sudden, definite presentment of a fiend.

"I thought it was madness," he said, as he replaced the obnoxious paper in the safe, "and now I begin to fear it is disgrace."

With that he blew out his candle, put on a greatcoat, and set forth in the direction of Cavendish Square, that citadel of medicine, where his friend, the great Dr. Lanyon, had his house and received his crowding patients. "If anyone knows, it will be Lanyon," he had thought.

The solemn butler knew and welcomed him; he was subjected to no stage of delay, but ushered direct from the door to the dining-room where Dr. Lanyon sat alone over his wine. This was a hearty, healthy, dapper, red-faced gentleman, with a shock of hair prematurely white, and a boisterous and decided manner. At sight of Mr. Utterson, he sprang up from his chair and welcomed him with both hands. The geniality, as was the way of the man, was somewhat theatrical to the eye; but it reposed on genuine feeling. For these two were old friends, old mates both at school and college, both thorough respectors of themselves and of each other, and what does not always follow, men who thoroughly enjoyed each other's company.

After a little rambling talk, the lawyer led up to the subject which so disagreeably preoccupied his mind.

"I suppose, Lanyon," said he, "you and I must be the two oldest friends that Henry Jekyll has?"

"I wish the friends were younger," chuckled Dr. Lanyon. "But I suppose we are. And what of that? I see little of him now."

"Indeed?" said Utterson. "I thought you had a bond of common interest."

"We had," was the reply. "But it is more than ten years since Henry Jekyll became too fanciful for me. He began to go wrong, wrong in mind; and though of course I continue to take an interest in him for old sake's sake, as they say, I see and I have seen devilish little of the man. Such unscientific balderdash," added the doctor, flushing suddenly purple, "would have estranged Damon and Pythias."

This little spirit of temper was somewhat of a relief to Mr. Utterson. "They have only differed on some point of science," he thought; and being a man of no scientific passions (except in the matter of conveyancing), he even added: "It is nothing worse than that!" He gave his friend a few seconds to recover his composure, and then approached the question he had come to put. "Did you ever come across a protégé of his—one Hyde?" he asked.

"Hyde?" repeated Lanyon. "No. Never heard of him. Since my time."

That was the amount of information that the lawyer carried back with him to the great, dark bed on which he tossed to and fro, until the small hours of the morning began to grow large. It was a night of little ease to his toiling mind, toiling in mere darkness and besieged by questions.

Six o'clock struck on the bells of the church that was so conveniently near to Mr. Utterson's dwelling, and still he was digging at the problem. Hitherto it had touched him on the intellectual side alone; but now his imagination also was engaged, or rather enslaved; and as he lay and tossed in the gross darkness of the night and the curtained room, Mr. Enfield's tale went by before his mind in a scroll of lighted pictures. He would be aware of the great field of lamps of a nocturnal city; then of the figure of a man walking swiftly; then of a child running from the doctor's; and then these met, and that human Juggernaut trod the child down and passed on regardless of her screams. Or else he would see a room in a rich house, where his friend lay asleep, dreaming and smiling at his dreams; and then the door of that room would be opened, the curtains of the bed plucked apart, the sleeper recalled, and lo! there would stand by his side a figure to whom power was given, and even at that dead hour, he must rise and do its bidding. The figure in these two phases haunted the lawyer all night; and if at any time he dozed over, it was but to see it glide more stealthily through sleeping houses, or move the more swiftly and still the more swiftly, even to dizziness, through wider labyrinths of lamplighted city, and at every street corner crush a child and leave her screaming. And still the figure had no face by which he might know it; even in his dreams, it had no face, or one that baffled him and melted before his eyes; and thus it was that there sprang up and grew apace in the lawyer's mind a singularly strong, almost an inordinate, curiosity to behold the features of the real Mr. Hyde. If he could but once set eyes on him, he thought the mystery would lighten and perhaps roll altogether away, as was the habit of mysterious things when well examined. He might see a reason for his friend's strange preference or bondage (call it which you please) and even for the startling clause of the will. At least it would be a face worth seeing: the face of a man who was without bowels of mercy: a face which had but to show itself to raise up, in the mind of the unimpressionable Enfield, a spirit of enduring hatred.

From that time forward, Mr. Utterson began to haunt the door in the by-street of shops. In the morning before office hours, at noon when business was plenty and time scarce, at night under the face of the fogged city moon, by all lights and at all hours of solitude or concourse, the lawyer was to be found on his chosen post.

"If he be Mr. Hyde," he had thought, "I shall be Mr. Seek."

And at last his patience was rewarded. It was a fine dry night; frost in the air; the streets as clean as a ballroom floor; the lamps, unshaken by any wind, drawing a regular pattern of light and shadow. By ten o'clock, when the shops were closed, the by-street was very solitary and, in spite of the low growl of London from all round, very silent. Small sounds carried far; domestic sounds out of the houses were clearly audible on either side of the roadway; and the rumour of the approach of any passenger preceded him by a long time. Mr. Utterson had been some minutes at his post, when he was aware of an odd light footstep drawing near. In the course of his nightly patrols, he had long grown accustomed to the quaint effect with which the footfalls of a single person, while he is still a great way off, suddenly spring out distinct from the vast hum and clatter of the city. Yet his attention had never before been so sharply and decisively arrested; and it was with a strong, superstitious prevision of success that he withdrew into the entry of the court.

The steps drew swiftly nearer, and swelled out suddenly louder as they turned the end of the street. The lawyer, looking forth from the entry, could soon see what manner of man he had to deal with. He was small and very plainly dressed and the look of him, even at that distance, went somehow strongly against the watcher's inclination. But he made straight for the door, crossing the roadway to save time; and as he came, he drew a key from his pocket like one approaching home.

Mr. Utterson stepped out and touched him on the shoulder as he passed. "Mr. Hyde, I think?"

Mr. Hyde shrank back with a hissing intake of the breath.

But his fear was only momentary; and though he did not look the lawyer in the face, he answered coolly enough:"That is my name. What do you want?"

"I see you are going in," returned the lawyer."I am an old friend of Dr. Jekyll's—Mr. Utterson of Gaunt Street—you must have heard of my name; and meeting you so conveniently, I thought you might admit me."

"You will not find Dr. Jekyll; he is from home," replied Mr. Hyde, blowing in the key. And then suddenly, but still without looking up,"How did you know me?"he asked.

"On your side,"said Mr. Utterson"will you do me a favour?"

"With pleasure,"replied the other."What shall it be?"

"Will you let me see your face?"asked the lawyer.

Mr. Hyde appeared to hesitate, and then, as if upon some sudden reflection, fronted about with an air of defiance; and the pair stared at each other pretty fixedly for a few seconds. "Now I shall know you again,"said Mr. Utterson. "It may be useful."

"Yes," returned Mr. Hyde, "It is as well we have met; and à propos, you should have my address." And he gave a number of a street in Soho.

"Good God!" thought Mr. Utterson, "can he, too, have been thinking of the will?" But he kept his feelings to himself and only grunted in acknowledgment of the address.

"And now," said the other, "how did you know me?"

"By description," was the reply.

"Whose description?"

"We have common friends," said Mr. Utterson.

"Common friends," echoed Mr. Hyde, a little hoarsely. "Who are they?"

"Jekyll, for instance," said the lawyer.

"He never told you," cried Mr. Hyde, with a flush of anger. "I did not think you would have lied."

"Come," said Mr. Utterson, "that is not fitting language."

The other snarled aloud into a savage laugh; and the next moment, with extraordinary quickness, he had unlocked the door and disappeared into the house.

The lawyer stood awhile when Mr. Hyde had left him, the picture of disquietude. Then he began slowly to mount the street, pausing every step or two and putting his hand to his brow like a man in mental perplexity. The problem he was thus debating as he walked, was one of a class that is rarely solved. Mr. Hyde was pale and dwarfish, he gave an impression of deformity without any nameable malformation, he had a displeasing smile, he had borne himself to the lawyer with a sort of murderous mixture of timidity and boldness, and he spoke with a husky, whispering and somewhat broken voice; all these were points against him, but not all of these together could explain the hitherto unknown disgust, loathing and fear with which Mr. Utterson regarded him. "There must be something else," said the perplexed gentleman. "There is something more, if I could find a name for it. God bless me, the man seems hardly human! Something troglodytic, shall we say? or can it be the old story of Dr. Fell? or is it the mere radiance of a foul soul that thus transpires through, and transfigures, its clay continent? The last, I think; for, O my poor old Harry Jekyll, if ever I read Satan's signature upon a face, it is on that of your new friend."

Round the corner from the by-street, there was a square of ancient, handsome houses, now for the most part decayed from their high estate and let in flats and chambers to all sorts and conditions of men; map-engravers, architects, shady lawyers and the agents of obscure enterprises. One house, however, second from the corner, was still occupied entire; and at the door of this, which wore a great air of wealth and comfort, though it was now plunged in darkness except for the fanlight, Mr. Utterson stopped and knocked. A well-dressed, elderly servant opened the door.

"Is Dr. Jekyll at home, Poole?" asked the lawyer.

"I will see, Mr. Utterson," said Poole, admitting the visitor, as he spoke, into a large, low-roofed, comfortable hall paved with flags, warmed (after the fashion of a country house) by a bright, open fire, and furnished with costly cabinets of oak. "Will you wait here by the fire, sir? or shall I give you a light in the dining-room?"

"Here, thank you," said the lawyer, and he drew near and leaned on the tall fender. This hall, in which he was now left alone, was a pet fancy of his friend the doctor's; and Utterson himself was wont to speak of it as the pleasantest room in London. But tonight there was a shudder in his blood; the face of Hyde sat heavy on his memory; he felt (what was rare with him) a nausea and distaste of life; and in the gloom of his spirits, he seemed to read a menace in the flickering of the firelight on the polished cabinets and the uneasy starting of the shadow on the roof. He was ashamed of his relief, when Poole presently returned to announce that Dr. Jekyll was gone out.

"I saw Mr. Hyde go in by the old dissecting room, Poole," he said. "Is that right, when Dr. Jekyll is from home?"

"Quite right, Mr. Utterson, sir," replied the servant. "Mr. Hyde has a key."

"Your master seems to repose a great deal of trust in that young man, Poole," resumed the other musingly.

"Yes, sir, he does indeed," said Poole. "We have all orders to obey him."

"I do not think I ever met Mr. Hyde?" asked Utterson.

"O, dear no, sir. He never dines here," replied the butler. "Indeed we see very little of him on this side of the house; he mostly comes and goes by the laboratory."

"Well, good-night, Poole."

"Good-night, Mr. Utterson."

And the lawyer set out homeward with a very heavy heart. "Poor Harry Jekyll," he thought, "my mind misgives me he is in deep waters! He was wild when he was young; a long while ago to be sure; but in the law of God, there is no statute of limitations. Ay, it must be that; the ghost of some old sin, the cancer of some concealed disgrace: punishment coming, pede claudo, years after memory has forgotten and self-love condoned the fault." And the lawyer, scared by the thought, brooded awhile on his own past, groping in all the corners of memory, least by chance some Jack-in-the-Box of an old iniquity should leap to light there. His past was fairly blameless; few men could read the rolls of their life with less apprehension; yet he was humbled to the dust by the many ill things he had done, and raised up again into a sober and fearful gratitude by the many he had come so near to doing yet avoided. And then by a return on his former subject, he conceived a spark of hope. "This Master Hyde, if he were studied," thought he, "must have secrets of his own; black secrets, by the look of him; secrets compared to which poor Jekyll's worst would be like sunshine. Things cannot continue as they are. It turns me cold to think of this creature stealing like a thief to Harry's bedside; poor Harry, what a wakening! And the danger of it; for if this Hyde suspects the existence of the will, he may grow impatient to inherit. Ay, I must put my shoulders to the wheel—if Jekyll will but let me," he added, "if Jekyll will only let me." For once more he saw before his mind's eye, as clear as transparency, the strange clauses of the will.

Chapter

Dr. Jekyll
Was Quite at Ease

03

I believe you fully; I would trust you before any man alive, ay,
before myself, if I could make the choice.

A fortnight later, by excellent good fortune, the doctor gave one of his pleasant dinners to some five or six old cronies, all intelligent, reputable men and all judges of good wine; and Mr. Utterson so contrived that he remained behind after the others had departed. This was no new arrangement, but a thing that had befallen many scores of times. Where Utterson was liked, he was liked well. Hosts loved to detain the dry lawyer, when the light-hearted and loose-tongued had already their foot on the threshold; they liked to sit a while in his unobtrusive company, practising for solitude, sobering their minds in the man's rich silence after the expense and strain of gaiety. To this rule, Dr. Jekyll was no exception; and as he now sat on the opposite side of the fire—a large, well-made, smooth-faced man of fifty, with something of a slyish cast perhaps, but every mark of capacity and kindness—you could see by his looks that he cherished for Mr. Utterson a sincere and warm affection.

"I have been wanting to speak to you, Jekyll," began the latter. "You know that will of yours?"

A close observer might have gathered that the topic was distasteful; but the doctor carried it off gaily. "My poor Utterson," said he, "you are unfortunate in such a client. I never saw a man so distressed as you were by my will; unless it were that hide-bound pedant, Lanyon, at what he called my scientific heresies. O, I know he's a good fellow—you needn't frown—an excellent fellow, and I always mean to see more of him; but a hide-bound pedant for all that; an ignorant, blatant pedant. I was never more disappointed in any man than Lanyon."

"You know I never approved of it," pursued Utterson, ruthlessly disregarding the fresh topic.

"My will? Yes, certainly, I know that," said the doctor, a trifle sharply. "You have told me so."

"Well, I tell you so again," continued the lawyer. "I have been learning something of young Hyde."

The large handsome face of Dr. Jekyll grew pale to the very lips, and there came a blackness about his eyes. "I do not care to hear more," said he. "This is a matter I thought we had agreed to drop."

"What I heard was abominable," said Utterson.

"It can make no change. You do not understand my position," returned the doctor, with a certain incoherency of manner. "I am painfully situated, Utterson; my position is a very strange—a very strange one. It is one of those affairs that cannot be mended by talking."

"Jekyll," said Utterson, "you know me: I am a man to be trusted. Make a clean breast of this in confidence; and I make no doubt I can get you out of it."

"My good Utterson," said the doctor, "this is very good of you, this is downright good of you, and I cannot find words to thank you in. I believe you fully; I would trust you before any man alive, ay, before myself, if I could make the choice; but indeed it isn't what you fancy; it is not as bad as that; and just to put your good heart at rest, I will tell you one thing: the moment I choose, I can be rid of Mr. Hyde. I give you my hand upon that; and I thank you again and again; and I will just add one little word, Utterson, that I'm sure you'll take in good part: this is a private matter, and I beg of you to let it sleep."

Utterson reflected a little, looking in the fire.

"I have no doubt you are perfectly right," he said at last, getting to his feet.

"Well, but since we have touched upon this business, and for the last time I hope," continued the doctor, "there is one point I should like you to understand. I have really a very great interest in poor Hyde. I know you have seen him; he told me so; and I fear he was rude. But I do sincerely take a great, a very great interest in that young man; and if I am taken away, Utterson, I wish you to promise me that you will bear with him and get his rights for him. I think you would, if you knew all; and it would be a weight off my mind if you would promise."

"I can't pretend that I shall ever like him," said the lawyer.

"I don't ask that," pleaded Jekyll, laying his hand upon the other's arm; "I only ask for justice; I only ask you to help him for my sake, when I am no longer here."

Utterson heaved an irrepressible sigh. "Well," said he, "I promise."

Chapter

The Carew Murder Case

04

She had an evil face, smoothed by hypocrisy:
but her manners were excellent.

Nearly a year later, in the month of October, 18—, London was startled by a crime of singular ferocity and rendered all the more notable by the high position of the victim. The details were few and startling. A maid servant living alone in a house not far from the river, had gone upstairs to bed about eleven. Although a fog rolled over the city in the small hours, the early part of the night was cloudless, and the lane, which the maid's window overlooked, was brilliantly lit by the full moon. It seems she was romantically given, for she sat down upon her box, which stood immediately under the window, and fell into a dream of musing. Never (she used to say, with streaming tears, when she narrated that experience), never had she felt more at peace with all men or thought more kindly of the world. And as she so sat she became aware of an aged beautiful gentleman with white hair, drawing near along the lane; and advancing to meet him, another and very small gentleman, to whom at first she paid less attention. When they had come within speech (which was just under the maid's eyes) the older man bowed and accosted the other with a very pretty manner of politeness. It did not seem as if the subject of his address were of great importance; indeed, from his pointing, it sometimes appeared as if he were only inquiring his way; but the moon shone on his face as he spoke, and the girl was pleased to watch it, it seemed to breathe such an innocent and old-world kindness of disposition, yet with something high too, as of a well-founded self-content. Presently her eye wandered to the other, and she was surprised to recognise in him a certain Mr. Hyde, who had once visited her master and for whom she had conceived a dislike. He had in his hand a heavy cane, with which he was trifling; but he answered never a word, and seemed to listen with an ill-contained impatience. And then all of a sudden he broke out in a great flame of anger, stamping with his foot, brandishing the cane, and carrying on (as the maid described it) like a madman. The old gentleman took a step back, with the air of one very much surprised and a trifle hurt; and at that Mr. Hyde broke out of all bounds and clubbed him to the earth. And next moment, with ape-like fury, he was trampling his victim under foot and hailing down a storm of blows, under which the bones were audibly shattered and the body jumped upon the roadway. At the horror of these sights and sounds, the maid fainted.

It was two o'clock when she came to herself and called for the police. The murderer was gone long ago; but there lay his victim in the middle of the lane, incredibly mangled. The stick with which the deed had been done, although it was of some rare and very tough and heavy wood, had broken in the middle under the stress of this insensate cruelty; and one splintered half had rolled in the neighbouring gutter—the other, without doubt, had been carried away by the murderer. A purse and gold watch were found upon the victim: but no cards or papers, except a sealed and stamped envelope, which he had been probably carrying to the post, and which bore the name and address of Mr. Utterson.

This was brought to the lawyer the next morning, before he was out of bed; and he had no sooner seen it and been told the circumstances, than he shot out a solemn lip. "I shall say nothing till I have seen the body," said he; "this may be very serious. Have the kindness to wait while I dress." And with the same grave countenance he hurried through his breakfast and drove to the police station, whither the body had been carried. As soon as he came into the cell, he nodded.

"Yes," said he, "I recognise him. I am sorry to say that this is Sir Danvers Carew."

"Good God, sir," exclaimed the officer, "is it possible?" And the next moment his eye lighted up with professional ambition. "This will make a deal of noise," he said. "And perhaps you can help us to the man." And he briefly narrated what the maid had seen, and showed the broken stick.

Mr. Utterson had already quailed at the name of Hyde; but when the stick was laid before him, he could doubt no longer;

broken and battered as it was, he recognised it for one that he had himself presented many years before to Henry Jekyll.

"Is this Mr. Hyde a person of small stature?" he inquired.

"Particularly small and particularly wicked-looking, is what the maid calls him," said the officer.

Mr. Utterson reflected; and then, raising his head, "If you will come with me in my cab," he said, "I think I can take you to his house."

It was by this time about nine in the morning, and the first fog of the season. A great chocolate-coloured pall lowered over heaven, but the wind was continually charging and routing these embattled vapours; so that as the cab crawled from street to street, Mr. Utterson beheld a marvelous number of degrees and hues of twilight; for here it would be dark like the back-end of evening; and there would be a glow of a rich, lurid brown, like the light of some strange conflagration; and here, for a moment, the fog would be quite broken up, and a haggard shaft of daylight would glance in between the swirling wreaths. The dismal quarter of Soho seen under these changing glimpses, with its muddy ways, and slatternly passengers, and its lamps, which had never been extinguished or had been kindled afresh to combat this mournful reinvasion of darkness, seemed, in the lawyer's eyes, like a district of some city in a nightmare. The thoughts of his mind, besides, were of the gloomiest dye; and when he glanced at the companion of his drive, he was conscious of some touch of that terror of the law and the law's officers, which may at times assail the most honest.

As the cab drew up before the address indicated, the fog lifted a little and showed him a dingy street, a gin palace, a low French eating house, a shop for the retail of penny numbers and twopenny salads, many ragged children huddled in the doorways, and many women of many different nationalities passing out, key in hand, to have a morning glass; and the next moment the fog settled down again upon that part, as brown as umber, and cut him off from his blackguardly surroundings. This was the home of Henry Jekyll's favourite; of a man who was heir to a quarter of a million sterling.

An ivory-faced and silvery-haired old woman opened the door. She had an evil face, smoothed by hypocrisy: but her manners were excellent. Yes, she said, this was Mr. Hyde's, but he was not at home; he had been in that night very late, but he had gone away again in less than an hour; there was nothing strange in that; his habits were very irregular, and he was often absent; for instance, it was nearly two months since she had seen him till yesterday.

"Very well, then, we wish to see his rooms," said the lawyer; and when the woman began to declare it was impossible, "I had better tell you who this person is," he added. "This is Inspector Newcomen of Scotland Yard."

A flash of odious joy appeared upon the woman's face. "Ah!" said she, "he is in trouble! What has he done?"

Mr. Utterson and the inspector exchanged glances. "He don't seem a very popular character," observed the latter. "And now, my good woman, just let me and this gentleman have a look about us."

In the whole extent of the house, which but for the old woman remained otherwise empty, Mr. Hyde had only used a couple of rooms; but these were furnished with luxury and good taste. A closet was filled with wine; the plate was of silver, the napery elegant; a good picture hung upon the walls, a gift (as Utterson supposed) from Henry Jekyll, who was much of a connoisseur; and the carpets were of many plies and agreeable in colour. At this moment, however, the rooms bore every mark of having been recently and hurriedly ransacked;

clothes lay about the floor, with their pockets inside out; lock-fast drawers stood open; and on the hearth there lay a pile of grey ashes, as though many papers had been burned. From these embers the inspector disinterred the butt end of a green cheque book, which had resisted the action of the fire; the other half of the stick was found behind the door; and as this clinched his suspicions, the officer declared himself delighted. A visit to the bank, where several thousand pounds were found to be lying to the murderer's credit, completed his gratification.

"You may depend upon it, sir," he told Mr. Utterson: "I have him in my hand. He must have lost his head, or he never would have left the stick or, above all, burned the cheque book. Why, money's life to the man. We have nothing to do but wait for him at the bank, and get out the handbills."

This last, however, was not so easy of accomplishment; for Mr. Hyde had numbered few familiars—even the master of the servant maid had only seen him twice; his family could nowhere be traced; he had never been photographed; and the few who could describe him differed widely, as common observers will. Only on one point were they agreed; and that was the haunting sense of unexpressed deformity with which the fugitive impressed his beholders.

Chapter

Incident of the Letter

05

The fog still slept on the wing above the drowned city,
where the lamps glimmered like carbuncles;
and through the muffle and smother of these fallen clouds,
the procession of the town's life was still rolling
in through the great arteries with a sound as of a mighty wind.

It was late in the afternoon, when Mr. Utterson found his way to Dr. Jekyll's door, where he was at once admitted by Poole, and carried down by the kitchen offices and across a yard which had once been a garden, to the building which was indifferently known as the laboratory or dissecting rooms. The doctor had bought the house from the heirs of a celebrated surgeon; and his own tastes being rather chemical than anatomical, had changed the destination of the block at the bottom of the garden. It was the first time that the lawyer had been received in that part of his friend's quarters; and he eyed the dingy, windowless structure with curiosity, and gazed round with a distasteful sense of strangeness as he crossed the theatre, once crowded with eager students and now lying gaunt and silent, the tables laden with chemical apparatus, the floor strewn with crates and littered with packing straw, and the light falling dimly through the foggy cupola. At the further end, a flight of stairs mounted to a door covered with red baize; and through this, Mr. Utterson was at last received into the doctor's cabinet. It was a large room fitted round with glass presses, furnished, among other things, with a cheval-glass and a business table, and looking out upon the court by three dusty windows barred with iron. The fire burned in the grate; a lamp was set lighted on the chimney shelf, for even in the houses the fog began to lie thickly; and there, close up to the warmth, sat Dr. Jekyll, looking deathly sick. He did not rise to meet his visitor, but held out a cold hand and bade him welcome in a changed voice.

"And now," said Mr. Utterson, as soon as Poole had left them, "you have heard the news?"

The doctor shuddered. "They were crying it in the square," he said. "I heard them in my dining-room."

"One word," said the lawyer. "Carew was my client, but so are you, and I want to know what I am doing. You have not been mad enough to hide this fellow?"

"Utterson, I swear to God," cried the doctor, "I swear to God I will never set eyes on him again. I bind my honour to you that I am done with him in this world. It is all at an end. And indeed he does not want my help; you do not know him as I do; he is safe, he is quite safe; mark my words, he will never more be heard of."

The lawyer listened gloomily; he did not like his friend's feverish manner. "You seem pretty sure of him," said he; "and for your sake, I hope you may be right. If it came to a trial, your name might appear."

"I am quite sure of him," replied Jekyll; "I have grounds for certainty that I cannot share with any one. But there is one thing on which you may advise me. I have—I have received a letter; and I am at a loss whether I should show it to the police. I should like to leave it in your hands, Utterson; you would judge wisely, I am sure; I have so great a trust in you."

"You fear, I suppose, that it might lead to his detection?" asked the lawyer.

"No," said the other. "I cannot say that I care what becomes of Hyde; I am quite done with him. I was thinking of my own character, which this hateful business has rather exposed."

Utterson ruminated awhile; he was surprised at his friend's selfishness, and yet relieved by it. "Well," said he, at last, "let me see the letter."

The letter was written in an odd, upright hand and signed "Edward Hyde": and it signified, briefly enough, that the writer's benefactor, Dr. Jekyll, whom he had long so unworthily repaid for a thousand generosities, need labour under no alarm for his safety, as he had means of escape on which he placed a sure dependence. The lawyer liked this letter well enough; it put a better colour on the intimacy than he had looked for; and he blamed himself for some of his past suspicions.

"Have you the envelope?" he asked.

"I burned it," replied Jekyll, "before I thought what I was about. But it bore no postmark. The note was handed in."

"Shall I keep this and sleep upon it?" asked Utterson.

"I wish you to judge for me entirely," was the reply. "I have lost confidence in myself."

"Well, I shall consider," returned the lawyer. "And now one word more: it was Hyde who dictated the terms in your will about that disappearance?"

The doctor seemed seized with a qualm of faintness; he shut his mouth tight and nodded.

"I knew it," said Utterson. "He meant to murder you. You have had a fine escape."

"I have had what is far more to the purpose," returned the doctor solemnly: "I have had a lesson—O God, Utterson, what a lesson I have had!" And he covered his face for a moment with his hands.

On his way out, the lawyer stopped and had a word or two with Poole.

"By the bye," said he, "there was a letter handed in to-day: what was the messenger like?" But Poole was positive nothing had come except by post; "and only circulars by that," he added.

This news sent off the visitor with his fears renewed. Plainly the letter had come by the laboratory door; possibly, indeed, it had been written in the cabinet; and if that were so, it must be differently judged, and handled with the more caution. The newsboys, as he went, were crying themselves hoarse along the footways: "Special edition. Shocking murder of an M.P." That was the funeral oration of one friend and client; and he could not help a certain apprehension lest the good name of another should be sucked down in the eddy of the scandal. It was, at least, a ticklish decision that he had to make; and self-reliant as he was by habit, he began to cherish a longing for advice. It was not to be had directly; but perhaps, he thought, it might be fished for.

Presently after, he sat on one side of his own hearth, with Mr. Guest, his head clerk, upon the other, and midway between, at a nicely calculated distance from the fire, a bottle of a particular old wine that had long dwelt unsunned in the foundations of his house. The fog still slept on the wing above the drowned city, where the lamps glimmered like carbuncles; and through the muffle and smother of these fallen clouds, the procession of the town's life was still rolling in through the great arteries with a sound as of a mighty wind. But the room was gay with firelight. In the bottle the acids were long ago resolved; the imperial dye had softened with time, as the colour grows richer in stained windows; and the glow of hot autumn afternoons on hillside vineyards, was ready to be set free and to disperse the fogs of London. Insensibly the lawyer melted. There was no man from whom he kept fewer secrets than Mr. Guest; and he was not always sure that he kept as many as he meant. Guest had often been on business to the doctor's; he knew Poole; he could scarce have failed to hear of Mr. Hyde's familiarity about the house; he might draw conclusions: was it not as well, then, that he should see a letter which put that mystery to right? and above all since Guest, being a great student and critic of handwriting, would consider the step natural and obliging? The clerk, besides, was a man of counsel; he could scarce read so strange a document without dropping a remark; and by that remark Mr. Utterson might shape his future course.

"This is a sad business about Sir Danvers," he said.

"Yes, sir, indeed. It has elicited a great deal of public feeling," returned Guest. "The man, of course, was mad."

"I should like to hear your views on that," replied Utterson. "I have a document here in his handwriting; it is between ourselves, for I scarce know what to do about it; it is an ugly business at the best. But there it is; quite in your way: a murderer's autograph."

Guest's eyes brightened, and he sat down at once and studied it with passion. "No, sir," he said: "not mad; but it is an odd hand."

"And by all accounts a very odd writer," added the lawyer.

Just then the servant entered with a note.

"Is that from Dr. Jekyll, sir?" inquired the clerk. "I thought I knew the writing. Anything private, Mr. Utterson?"

"Only an invitation to dinner. Why? Do you want to see it?"

"One moment. I thank you, sir;" and the clerk laid the two

sheets of paper alongside and sedulously compared their contents. "Thank you, sir," he said at last, returning both; "it's a
very interesting autograph."

There was a pause, during which Mr. Utterson struggled
with himself. "Why did you compare them, Guest?" he inquired suddenly.

"Well, sir," returned the clerk, "there's a rather singular resemblance; the two hands are in many points identical: only
differently sloped."

"Rather quaint," said Utterson.

"It is, as you say, rather quaint," returned Guest.

"I wouldn't speak of this note, you know," said the master.

"No, sir," said the clerk. "I understand."

But no sooner was Mr. Utterson alone that night, than he
locked the note into his safe, where it reposed from that time
forward. "What!" he thought. "Henry Jekyll forge for a murderer!" And his blood ran cold in his veins.

Chapter

Remarkable Incident of Dr. Lanyon

06

I sat in the sun on a bench; the animal within me
licking the chops of memory; the spiritual side a little drowsed,
promising subsequent penitence, but not yet moved to begin.

Time ran on; thousands of pounds were offered in reward, for the death of Sir Danvers was resented as a public injury; but Mr. Hyde had disappeared out of the ken of the police as though he had never existed. Much of his past was un-earthed, indeed, and all disreputable: tales came out of the man's cruelty, at once so callous and violent; of his vile life, of his strange associates, of the hatred that seemed to have surrounded his career; but of his present whereabouts, not a whisper. From the time he had left the house in Soho on the morning of the murder, he was simply blotted out; and grad-ually, as time drew on, Mr. Utterson began to recover from the hotness of his alarm, and to grow more at quiet with himself. The death of Sir Danvers was, to his way of thinking, more than paid for by the disappearance of Mr. Hyde. Now that that evil influence had been withdrawn, a new life began for Dr. Jekyll. He came out of his seclusion, renewed relations with his friends, became once more their familiar guest and en-tertainer; and whilst he had always been known for charities, he was now no less distinguished for religion. He was busy, he was much in the open air, he did good; his face seemed to open and brighten, as if with an inward consciousness of ser-vice; and for more than two months, the doctor was at peace.

On the 8th of January Utterson had dined at the doctor's with a small party; Lanyon had been there; and the face of the host had looked from one to the other as in the old days when the trio were inseparable friends. On the 12th, and again on the 14th, the door was shut against the lawyer. "The doctor was confined to the house," Poole said, "and saw no one." On the 15th, he tried again, and was again refused; and having now been used for the last two months to see his friend almost daily, he found this return of solitude to weigh upon his spirits. The fifth night he had in Guest to dine with him; and the sixth he betook himself to Dr. Lanyon's.

There at least he was not denied admittance; but when he came in, he was shocked at the change which had taken place in the doctor's appearance. He had his death-warrant written legibly upon his face. The rosy man had grown pale; his flesh had fallen away; he was visibly balder and older; and yet it was not so much these tokens of a swift physical decay that arrested the lawyer's notice, as a look in the eye and quality of manner that seemed to testify to some deep-seated terror of the mind. It was unlikely that the doctor should fear death; and yet that was what Utterson was tempted to suspect. "Yes," he thought; "he is a doctor, he must know his own state and that his days are counted; and the knowledge is more than he can bear." And yet when Utterson remarked on his ill looks, it was with an air of great firmness that Lanyon declared himself a doomed man.

"I have had a shock," he said, "and I shall never recover. It is a question of weeks. Well, life has been pleasant; I liked it; yes, sir, I used to like it. I sometimes think if we knew all, we should be more glad to get away."

"Jekyll is ill, too," observed Utterson. "Have you seen him?"

But Lanyon's face changed, and he held up a trembling hand. "I wish to see or hear no more of Dr. Jekyll," he said in a loud, unsteady voice. "I am quite done with that person; and I beg that you will spare me any allusion to one whom I regard as dead."

"Tut, tut!" said Mr. Utterson; and then after a considerable pause, "Can't I do anything?" he inquired. "We are three very old friends, Lanyon; we shall not live to make others."

"Nothing can be done," returned Lanyon; "ask himself."

"He will not see me," said the lawyer.

"I am not surprised at that," was the reply. "Some day, Utterson, after I am dead, you may perhaps come to learn the right and wrong of this. I cannot tell you. And in the meantime, if you can sit and talk with me of other things, for God's sake, stay and do so; but if you cannot keep clear of this accursed topic, then in God's name, go, for I cannot bear it."

As soon as he got home, Utterson sat down and wrote to Jekyll, complaining of his exclusion from the house, and asking the cause of this unhappy break with Lanyon; and the next day brought him a long answer, often very pathetically worded, and sometimes darkly mysterious in drift. The quarrel with Lanyon was incurable. "I do not blame our old friend," Jekyll wrote, "but I share his view that we must never meet. I mean from henceforth to lead a life of extreme seclusion; you must not be surprised, nor must you doubt my friendship, if my door is often shut even to you. You must suffer me to go my own dark way. I have brought on myself a punishment and a danger that I cannot name. If I am the chief of sinners, I am the chief of sufferers also. I could not think that this earth contained a place for sufferings and terrors so unmanning; and you can do but one thing, Utterson, to lighten this destiny, and that is to respect my silence." Utterson was amazed; the dark influence of Hyde had been withdrawn, the doctor had returned to his old tasks and amities; a week ago, the prospect had smiled with every promise of a cheerful and an honoured age; and now in a moment, friendship, and peace of mind, and the whole tenor of his life were wrecked. So great and unprepared a change pointed to madness; but in view of

Lanyon's manner and words, there must lie for it some deeper ground.

A week afterwards Dr. Lanyon took to his bed, and in something less than a fortnight he was dead. The night after the funeral, at which he had been sadly affected, Utterson locked the door of his business room, and sitting there by the light of a melancholy candle, drew out and set before him an envelope addressed by the hand and sealed with the seal of his dead friend. "PRIVATE: for the hands of G. J. Utterson ALONE, and in case of his predecease to be destroyed un-read," so it was emphatically superscribed; and the lawyer dreaded to behold the contents. "I have buried one friend to-day," he thought: "what if this should cost me another?" And then he condemned the fear as a disloyalty, and broke the seal. Within there was another enclosure, likewise sealed, and marked upon the cover as "not to be opened till the death or disappearance of Dr. Henry Jekyll." Utterson could not trust his eyes. Yes, it was disappearance; here again, as in the mad will which he had long ago restored to its author, here again were the idea of a disappearance and the name of Henry Jekyll bracketted. But in the will, that idea had sprung from the sinister suggestion of the man Hyde; it was set there with a purpose all too plain and horrible. Written by the hand of Lanyon, what should it mean? A great curiosity came on the trustee, to disregard the prohibition and dive at once to the bottom of these mysteries; but professional honour and faith to his dead friend were stringent obligations; and the packet slept in the inmost corner of his private safe.

It is one thing to mortify curiosity, another to conquer it; and it may be doubted if, from that day forth, Utterson desired the society of his surviving friend with the same eagerness. He thought of him kindly; but his thoughts were disquieted and fearful. He went to call indeed; but he was perhaps relieved to be denied admittance; perhaps, in his heart, he preferred to speak with Poole upon the doorstep and surrounded by the air and sounds of the open city, rather than to be admitted into that house of voluntary bondage, and to sit and speak with its inscrutable recluse. Poole had, indeed, no very pleasant news to communicate. The doctor, it appeared, now more than ever confined himself to the cabinet over the laboratory, where he would sometimes even sleep; he was out of spirits, he had grown very silent, he did not read; it seemed as if he had something on his mind. Utterson became so used to the unvarying character of these reports, that he fell off little by little in the frequency of his visits.

Chapter

Incident at the Window

07

That story's at an end at least.
We shall never see more of Mr. Hyde.

It chanced on Sunday, when Mr. Utterson was on his usual walk with Mr. Enfield, that their way lay once again through the by-street; and that when they came in front of the door, both stopped to gaze on it.

"Well," said Enfield, "that story's at an end at least. We shall never see more of Mr. Hyde."

"I hope not," said Utterson. "Did I ever tell you that I once saw him, and shared your feeling of repulsion?"

"It was impossible to do the one without the other," returned Enfield. "And by the way, what an ass you must have thought me, not to know that this was a back way to Dr. Jekyll's! It was partly your own fault that I found it out, even when I did."

"So you found it out, did you?" said Utterson. "But if that be so, we may step into the court and take a look at the windows. To tell you the truth, I am uneasy about poor Jekyll; and even outside, I feel as if the presence of a friend might do him good."

The court was very cool and a little damp, and full of premature twilight, although the sky, high up overhead, was still bright with sunset. The middle one of the three windows was half-way open; and sitting close beside it, taking the air with an infinite sadness of mien, like some disconsolate prisoner, Utterson saw Dr. Jekyll.

"What! Jekyll!" he cried. "I trust you are better."

"I am very low, Utterson," replied the doctor drearily, "very low. It will not last long, thank God."

"You stay too much indoors," said the lawyer. "You should be out, whipping up the circulation like Mr. Enfield and me. (This is my cousin—Mr. Enfield—Dr. Jekyll.) Come now; get your hat and take a quick turn with us."

"You are very good," sighed the other. "I should like to very much; but no, no, no, it is quite impossible; I dare not. But indeed, Utterson, I am very glad to see you; this is really a great pleasure; I would ask you and Mr. Enfield up, but the place is really not fit."

"Why, then," said the lawyer, good-naturedly, "the best thing we can do is to stay down here and speak with you from where we are."

"That is just what I was about to venture to propose," returned the doctor with a smile. But the words were hardly uttered, before the smile was struck out of his face and succeeded by an expression of such abject terror and despair, as froze the very blood of the two gentlemen below. They saw it but for a glimpse for the window was instantly thrust down; but that glimpse had been sufficient, and they turned and left the court without a word. In silence, too, they traversed the by-street; and it was not until they had come into a neighbouring thoroughfare, where even upon a Sunday there were still some stirrings of life, that Mr. Utterson at last turned and looked at his companion. They were both pale; and there was an answering horror in their eyes.

"God forgive us, God forgive us," said Mr. Utterson.

But Mr. Enfield only nodded his head very seriously, and walked on once more in silence.

Chapter

The Last Night

08

This suspense, I know, is telling upon all of you;
but it is now our intention to make an end of it.

Mr. Utterson was sitting by his fireside one evening after dinner, when he was surprised to receive a visit from Poole.

"Bless me, Poole, what brings you here?" he cried; and then taking a second look at him, "What ails you?" he added; "is the doctor ill?"

"Mr. Utterson," said the man, "there is something wrong."

"Take a seat, and here is a glass of wine for you," said the lawyer. "Now, take your time, and tell me plainly what you want."

"You know the doctor's ways, sir," replied Poole, "and how he shuts himself up. Well, he's shut up again in the cabinet; and I don't like it, sir—I wish I may die if I like it. Mr. Utterson, sir, I'm afraid."

"Now, my good man," said the lawyer, "be explicit. What are you afraid of?"

"I've been afraid for about a week," returned Poole, doggedly disregarding the question, "and I can bear it no more."

The man's appearance amply bore out his words; his manner was altered for the worse; and except for the moment when he had first announced his terror, he had not once looked the lawyer in the face. Even now, he sat with the glass of wine untasted on his knee, and his eyes directed to a corner of the floor. "I can bear it no more," he repeated.

"Come," said the lawyer, "I see you have some good reason, Poole; I see there is something seriously amiss. Try to tell me what it is."

"I think there's been foul play," said Poole, hoarsely.

"Foul play!" cried the lawyer, a good deal frightened and rather inclined to be irritated in consequence. "What foul play! What does the man mean?"

"I daren't say, sir," was the answer; "but will you come along with me and see for yourself?"

Mr. Utterson's only answer was to rise and get his hat and greatcoat; but he observed with wonder the greatness of the relief that appeared upon the butler's face, and perhaps with no less, that the wine was still untasted when he set it down to follow.

It was a wild, cold, seasonable night of March, with a pale moon, lying on her back as though the wind had tilted her, and flying wrack of the most diaphanous and lawny texture. The wind made talking difficult, and flecked the blood into the face. It seemed to have swept the streets unusually bare of passengers, besides; for Mr. Utterson thought he had never seen that part of London so deserted. He could have wished it otherwise; never in his life had he been conscious of so sharp a wish to see and touch his fellow-creatures; for struggle as he might, there was borne in upon his mind a crushing anticipation of calamity. The square, when they got there, was full of wind and dust, and the thin trees in the garden were lashing themselves along the railing. Poole, who had kept all the way a pace or two ahead, now pulled up in the middle of the pavement, and in spite of the biting weather, took off his hat and mopped his brow with a red pocket-handkerchief. But for all the hurry of his coming, these were not the dews of exertion that he wiped away, but the moisture of some strangling anguish; for his face was white and his voice, when he spoke, harsh and broken.

"Well, sir," he said, "here we are, and God grant there be nothing wrong."

"Amen, Poole," said the lawyer.

Thereupon the servant knocked in a very guarded manner; the door was opened on the chain; and a voice asked from within, "Is that you, Poole?"

"It's all right," said Poole. "Open the door."

The hall, when they entered it, was brightly lighted up; the fire was built high; and about the hearth the whole of the servants, men and women, stood huddled together like a flock of sheep. At the sight of Mr. Utterson, the housemaid broke into hysterical whimpering; and the cook, crying out "Bless God! it's Mr. Utterson," ran forward as if to take him in her arms.

"What, what? Are you all here?" said the lawyer peevishly. "Very irregular, very unseemly; your master would be far from pleased."

"They're all afraid," said Poole.

Blank silence followed, no one protesting; only the maid lifted her voice and now wept loudly.

"Hold your tongue!" Poole said to her, with a ferocity of accent that testified to his own jangled nerves; and indeed, when the girl had so suddenly raised the note of her lamentation, they had all started and turned towards the inner door with faces of dreadful expectation. "And now," continued the butler, addressing the knife-boy, "reach me a candle, and we'll get this through hands at once." And then he begged Mr. Utterson to follow him, and led the way to the back garden.

"Now, sir," said he, "you come as gently as you can. I want you to hear, and I don't want you to be heard. And see here, sir, if by any chance he was to ask you in, don't go."

Mr. Utterson's nerves, at this unlooked-for termination, gave a jerk that nearly threw him from his balance; but he recollected his courage and followed the butler into the laboratory building through the surgical theatre, with its lumber of crates and bottles, to the foot of the stair. Here Poole motioned him to stand on one side and listen; while he himself, setting down the candle and making a great and obvious call on his resolution, mounted the steps and knocked with a somewhat uncertain hand on the red baize of the cabinet door.

"Mr. Utterson, sir, asking to see you," he called; and even as he did so, once more violently signed to the lawyer to give ear.

A voice answered from within: "Tell him I cannot see anyone," it said complainingly.

"Thank you, sir," said Poole, with a note of something like triumph in his voice; and taking up his candle, he led Mr. Utterson back across the yard and into the great kitchen, where the fire was out and the beetles were leaping on the floor.

"Sir," he said, looking Mr. Utterson in the eyes, "Was that my master's voice?"

"It seems much changed," replied the lawyer, very pale, but giving look for look.

"Changed? Well, yes, I think so," said the butler. "Have I been twenty years in this man's house, to be deceived about his voice? No, sir; master's made away with; he was made away with eight days ago, when we heard him cry out upon the name of God; and who's in there instead of him, and why it stays there, is a thing that cries to Heaven, Mr. Utterson!"

"This is a very strange tale, Poole; this is rather a wild tale, my man," said Mr. Utterson, biting his finger. "Suppose it were as you suppose, supposing Dr. Jekyll to have been—well, murdered, what could induce the murderer to stay? That won't hold water; it doesn't commend itself to reason."

"Well, Mr. Utterson, you are a hard man to satisfy, but I'll do it yet," said Poole. "All this last week (you must know) him, or it, whatever it is that lives in that cabinet, has been crying night and day for some sort of medicine and cannot get it to his mind. It was sometimes his way—the master's, that is—to write his orders on a sheet of paper and throw it on the stair. We've had nothing else this week back; nothing but papers, and a closed door, and the very meals left there to be smuggled in when nobody was looking. Well, sir, every day, ay, and twice and thrice in the same day, there have been orders and complaints, and I have been sent flying to all the wholesale chemists in town. Every time I brought the stuff back, there would be another paper telling me to return it, because it was not pure, and another order to a different firm. This drug is wanted bitter bad, sir, whatever for."

"Have you any of these papers?" asked Mr. Utterson.

Poole felt in his pocket and handed out a crumpled note, which the lawyer, bending nearer to the candle, carefully examined. Its contents ran thus: "Dr. Jekyll presents his compliments to Messrs. Maw. He assures them that their last sample is impure and quite useless for his present purpose. In the year 18—, Dr. J. purchased a somewhat large quantity from Messrs. M. He now begs them to search with most sedulous care, and should any of the same quality be left, forward it to him at once. Expense is no consideration. The importance of this to Dr. J. can hardly be exaggerated." So far the letter had run composedly enough, but here with a sudden splutter of the pen, the writer's emotion had broken loose. "For God's sake," he added, "find me some of the old."

"This is a strange note," said Mr. Utterson; and then sharply, "How do you come to have it open?"

"The man at Maw's was main angry, sir, and he threw it back to me like so much dirt," returned Poole.

"This is unquestionably the doctor's hand, do you know?" resumed the lawyer.

"I thought it looked like it," said the servant rather sulkily; and then, with another voice, "But what matters hand of write?" he said. "I've seen him!"

"Seen him?" repeated Mr. Utterson. "Well?"

"That's it!" said Poole. "It was this way. I came suddenly into the theatre from the garden. It seems he had slipped out to look for this drug or whatever it is; for the cabinet door was open, and there he was at the far end of the room digging among the crates. He looked up when I came in, gave a kind of cry, and whipped upstairs into the cabinet. It was but for one minute that I saw him, but the hair stood upon my head like quills. Sir, if that was my master, why had he a mask upon his face? If it was my master, why did he cry out like a rat, and run from me? I have served him long enough. And then..."The man paused and passed his hand over his face.

"These are all very strange circumstances," said Mr. Utterson, "but I think I begin to see daylight. Your master, Poole, is plainly seized with one of those maladies that both torture and deform the sufferer; hence, for aught I know, the alteration of his voice; hence the mask and the avoidance of his friends; hence his eagerness to find this drug, by means of which the poor soul retains some hope of ultimate recovery—God grant that he be not deceived! There is my explanation; it is sad enough, Poole, ay, and appalling to consider; but it is plain and natural, hangs well together, and delivers us from all exorbitant alarms."

"Sir," said the butler, turning to a sort of mottled pallor, "that thing was not my master, and there's the truth. My master"—here he looked round him and began to whisper—"is a tall, fine build of a man, and this was more of a dwarf." Utterson attempted to protest. "O, sir," cried Poole, "do you think I do not know my master after twenty years? Do you think I do not know where his head comes to in the cabinet door, where I saw him every morning of my life? No, sir, that thing in the mask was never Dr. Jekyll—God knows what it was, but it was never Dr. Jekyll; and it is the belief of my heart that there was murder done."

"Poole," replied the lawyer, "if you say that, it will become my duty to make certain. Much as I desire to spare your master's feelings, much as I am puzzled by this note which seems to prove him to be still alive, I shall consider it my duty to break in that door."

"Ah, Mr. Utterson, that's talking!" cried the butler.

"And now comes the second question," resumed Utterson: "Who is going to do it?"

"Why, you and me, sir," was the undaunted reply.

"That's very well said," returned the lawyer; "and whatever comes of it, I shall make it my business to see you are no loser."

"There is an axe in the theatre," continued Poole; "and you might take the kitchen poker for yourself."

The lawyer took that rude but weighty instrument into his hand, and balanced it. "Do you know, Poole," he said, looking up, "that you and I are about to place ourselves in a position of some peril?"

"You may say so, sir, indeed," returned the butler.

"It is well, then that we should be frank," said the other. "We both think more than we have said; let us make a clean breast. This masked figure that you saw, did you recognise it?"

"Well, sir, it went so quick, and the creature was so doubled up, that I could hardly swear to that," was the answer. "But if you mean, was it Mr. Hyde?—why, yes, I think it was! You see, it was much of the same bigness; and it had the same quick, light way with it; and then who else could have got in by the laboratory door? You have not forgot, sir, that at the time of the murder he had still the key with him? But that's not all. I don't know, Mr. Utterson, if you ever met this Mr. Hyde?"

"Yes," said the lawyer, "I once spoke with him."

"Then you must know as well as the rest of us that there was something queer about that gentleman—something that gave a man a turn—I don't know rightly how to say it, sir, beyond this: that you felt in your marrow kind of cold and thin."

"I own I felt something of what you describe," said Mr. Utterson.

"Quite so, sir," returned Poole. "Well, when that masked thing like a monkey jumped from among the chemicals and whipped into the cabinet, it went down my spine like ice. O, I know it's not evidence, Mr. Utterson; I'm book-learned enough for that; but a man has his feelings, and I give you my bible-word it was Mr. Hyde!"

"Ay, ay," said the lawyer. "My fears incline to the same point. Evil, I fear, founded—evil was sure to come—of that connection. Ay truly, I believe you; I believe poor Harry is killed; and I believe his murderer (for what purpose, God alone can tell) is still lurking in his victim's room. Well, let our name be vengeance. Call Bradshaw."

The footman came at the summons, very white and nervous.

"Pull yourself together, Bradshaw," said the lawyer. "This suspense, I know, is telling upon all of you; but it is now our intention to make an end of it. Poole, here, and I are going to force our way into the cabinet. If all is well, my shoulders are broad enough to bear the blame. Meanwhile, lest anything should really be amiss, or any malefactor seek to escape by the back, you and the boy must go round the corner with a pair of good sticks and take your post at the laboratory door. We give you ten minutes to get to your stations."

As Bradshaw left, the lawyer looked at his watch. "And now, Poole, let us get to ours," he said; and taking the poker under his arm, led the way into the yard. The scud had banked over the moon, and it was now quite dark. The wind, which only broke in puffs and draughts into that deep well of building, tossed the light of the candle to and fro about their steps, until they came into the shelter of the theatre, where they sat down silently to wait. London hummed solemnly all around; but nearer at hand, the stillness was only broken by the sound of a footfall moving to and fro along the cabinet floor.

"So it will walk all day, sir," whispered Poole; "ay, and the better part of the night. Only when a new sample comes from the chemist, there's a bit of a break. Ah, it's an ill conscience that's such an enemy to rest! Ah, sir, there's blood foully shed in every step of it! But hark again, a little closer—put your heart in your ears, Mr. Utterson, and tell me, is that the doctor's foot?"

The steps fell lightly and oddly, with a certain swing, for all they went so slowly; it was different indeed from the heavy creaking tread of Henry Jekyll. Utterson sighed. "Is there never anything else?" he asked.

Poole nodded. "Once," he said. "Once I heard it weeping!"

"Weeping? how that?" said the lawyer, conscious of a sudden chill of horror.

"Weeping like a woman or a lost soul," said the butler. "I came away with that upon my heart, that I could have wept too."

But now the ten minutes drew to an end. Poole disinterred the axe from under a stack of packing straw; the candle was set upon the nearest table to light them to the attack; and they drew near with bated breath to where that patient foot was still going up and down, up and down, in the quiet of the night.

"Jekyll," cried Utterson, with a loud voice, "I demand to see you." He paused a moment, but there came no reply. "I give you fair warning, our suspicions are aroused, and I must and shall see you," he resumed; "if not by fair means, then by foul—if not of your consent, then by brute force!"

"Utterson," said the voice, "for God's sake, have mercy!"

"Ah, that's not Jekyll's voice—it's Hyde's!" cried Utterson. "Down with the door, Poole!"

Poole swung the axe over his shoulder; the blow shook the building, and the red baize door leaped against the lock and hinges. A dismal screech, as of mere animal terror, rang from the cabinet. Up went the axe again, and again the panels crashed and the frame bounded; four times the blow fell; but the wood was tough and the fittings were of excellent work-manship; and it was not until the fifth, that the lock burst and the wreck of the door fell inwards on the carpet.

The besiegers, appalled by their own riot and the stillness that had succeeded, stood back a little and peered in. There lay the cabinet before their eyes in the quiet lamplight, a good fire glowing and chattering on the hearth, the kettle singing its thin strain, a drawer or two open, papers neatly set forth on the business table, and nearer the fire, the things laid out for tea; the quietest room, you would have said, and, but for the glazed presses full of chemicals, the most commonplace that night in London.

Right in the middle there lay the body of a man sorely contorted and still twitching. They drew near on tiptoe, turned it on its back and beheld the face of Edward Hyde. He was dressed in clothes far too large for him, clothes of the doctor's bigness; the cords of his face still moved with a semblance of life, but life was quite gone; and by the crushed phial in the hand and the strong smell of kernels that hung upon the air, Utterson knew that he was looking on the body of a self-destroyer.

"We have come too late," he said sternly, "whether to save or punish. Hyde is gone to his account; and it only remains for us to find the body of your master."

The far greater proportion of the building was occupied by the theatre, which filled almost the whole ground storey and was lighted from above, and by the cabinet, which formed an upper storey at one end and looked upon the court. A corridor joined the theatre to the door on the by-street; and with this the cabinet communicated separately by a second flight of stairs. There were besides a few dark closets and a spacious cellar. All these they now thoroughly examined. Each closet needed but a glance, for all were empty, and all, by the dust that fell from their doors, had stood long unopened. The cellar, indeed, was filled with crazy lumber, mostly dating from the times of the surgeon who was Jekyll's predecessor; but even as they opened the door they were advertised of the uselessness of further search, by the fall of a perfect mat of cobweb which had for years sealed up the entrance. Nowhere was there any trace of Henry Jekyll, dead or alive.

Poole stamped on the flags of the corridor. "He must be buried here," he said, hearkening to the sound.

"Or he may have fled," said Utterson, and he turned to examine the door in the by-street. It was locked; and lying near by on the flags, they found the key, already stained with rust. "This does not look like use," observed the lawyer.

"Use!" echoed Poole. "Do you not see, sir, it is broken? much as if a man had stamped on it."

"Ay," continued Utterson, "and the fractures, too, are rusty." The two men looked at each other with a scare. "This is beyond me, Poole," said the lawyer. "Let us go back to the cabinet."

They mounted the stair in silence, and still with an occasional awestruck glance at the dead body, proceeded more thoroughly to examine the contents of the cabinet. At one table, there were traces of chemical work, various measured heaps of some white salt being laid on glass saucers, as though for an experiment in which the unhappy man had been prevented.

"That is the same drug that I was always bringing him," said Poole; and even as he spoke, the kettle with a startling noise boiled over.

This brought them to the fireside, where the easy-chair was drawn cosily up, and the tea things stood ready to the sitter's elbow, the very sugar in the cup. There were several books on a shelf; one lay beside the tea things open, and Utterson was amazed to find it a copy of a pious work, for which Jekyll had several times expressed a great esteem, annotated, in his own hand with startling blasphemies.

Next, in the course of their review of the chamber, the searchers came to the cheval-glass, into whose depths they looked with an involuntary horror. But it was so turned as to show them nothing but the rosy glow playing on the roof, the fire sparkling in a hundred repetitions along the glazed front of the presses, and their own pale and fearful countenances stooping to look in.

"This glass has seen some strange things, sir," whispered Poole.

"And surely none stranger than itself," echoed the lawyer in the same tones. "For what did Jekyll"—he caught himself up at the word with a start, and then conquering the weakness—"what could Jekyll want with it?" he said.

"You may say that!" said Poole.

Next they turned to the business table. On the desk, among the neat array of papers, a large envelope was uppermost, and bore, in the doctor's hand, the name of Mr. Utterson. The lawyer unsealed it, and several enclosures fell to the floor. The first was a will, drawn in the same eccentric terms as the one which he had returned six months before, to serve as a testament in case of death and as a deed of gift in case of disappearance; but in place of the name of Edward Hyde, the lawyer, with indescribable amazement read the name of Gabriel John Utterson. He looked at Poole, and then back at the paper, and last of all at the dead malefactor stretched upon the carpet.

"My head goes round," he said. "He has been all these days in possession; he had no cause to like me; he must have raged to see himself displaced; and he has not destroyed this document."

He caught up the next paper; it was a brief note in the doctor's hand and dated at the top. "O Poole!" the lawyer cried, "he was alive and here this day. He cannot have been disposed of in so short a space; he must be still alive, he must have fled! And then, why fled? and how? and in that case, can we venture to declare this suicide? O, we must be careful. I foresee that we may yet involve your master in some dire catastrophe."

"Why don't you read it, sir?" asked Poole.

"Because I fear," replied the lawyer solemnly. "God grant I have no cause for it!" And with that he brought the paper to his eyes and read as follows:

"My dear Utterson,—When this shall fall into your hands, I shall have disappeared, under what circumstances I have not

the penetration to foresee, but my instinct and all the circumstances of my nameless situation tell me that the end is sure
and must be early. Go then, and first read the narrative which
Lanyon warned me he was to place in your hands; and if you
care to hear more, turn to the confession of

"Your unworthy and unhappy friend,

"HENRY JEKYLL."

"There was a third enclosure?" asked Utterson.

"Here, sir," said Poole, and gave into his hands a considerable packet sealed in several places.

The lawyer put it in his pocket. "I would say nothing of this
paper. If your master has fled or is dead, we may at least save
his credit. It is now ten; I must go home and read these docu-
ments in quiet; but I shall be back before midnight, when we
shall send for the police."

They went out, locking the door of the theatre behind them;
and Utterson, once more leaving the servants gathered about
the fire in the hall, trudged back to his office to read the two
narratives in which this mystery was now to be explained.

Chapter

Dr. Lanyon's Narrative

09

The less I understood of this farrago,
the less I was in a position to judge of its importance.

On the ninth of January, now four days ago, I received by the evening delivery a registered envelope, addressed in the hand of my colleague and old school companion, Henry Jekyll. I was a good deal surprised by this; for we were by no means in the habit of correspondence; I had seen the man, dined with him, indeed, the night before; and I could imagine nothing in our intercourse that should justify formality of registration. The contents increased my wonder; for this is how the letter ran:

"10th December, 18—.

"Dear Lanyon,—You are one of my oldest friends; and although we may have differed at times on scientific questions, I cannot remember, at least on my side, any break in our affection. There was never a day when, if you had said to me, 'Jekyll, my life, my honour, my reason, depend upon you,' I would not have sacrificed my left hand to help you. Lanyon, my life, my honour, my reason, are all at your mercy; if you fail me to-night, I am lost. You might suppose, after this preface, that I am going to ask you for something dishonourable to grant. Judge for yourself.

"I want you to postpone all other engagements for to-night—ay, even if you were summoned to the bedside of an emperor; to take a cab, unless your carriage should be actually at the door; and with this letter in your hand for consultation, to drive straight to my house. Poole, my butler, has his orders; you will find him waiting your arrival with a locksmith. The door of my cabinet is then to be forced; and you are to go in alone; to open the glazed press (letter E) on the left hand, breaking the lock if it be shut; and to draw out, with all its contents as they stand, the fourth drawer from the top or (which is the same thing) the third from the bottom. In my extreme distress of mind, I have a morbid fear of misdirecting you; but even if I am in error, you may know the right drawer by its contents: some powders, a phial and a paper book. This drawer I beg of you to carry back with you to Cavendish Square exactly as it stands.

"That is the first part of the service: now for the second. You should be back, if you set out at once on the receipt of this, long before midnight; but I will leave you that amount of margin, not only in the fear of one of those obstacles that can neither be prevented nor foreseen, but because an hour when your servants are in bed is to be preferred for what will then remain to do. At midnight, then, I have to ask you to be alone in your consulting room, to admit with your own hand into the house a man who will present himself in my name, and to place in his hands the drawer that you will have brought with you from my cabinet. Then you will have played your part and earned my gratitude completely. Five minutes afterwards, if you insist upon an explanation, you will have understood that these arrangements are of capital importance; and that by the neglect of one of them, fantastic as they must appear, you might have charged your conscience with my death or the shipwreck of my reason.

"Confident as I am that you will not trifle with this appeal, my heart sinks and my hand trembles at the bare thought of such a possibility. Think of me at this hour, in a strange place, labouring under a blackness of distress that no fancy can exaggerate, and yet well aware that, if you will but punctually serve me, my troubles will roll away like a story that is told. Serve me, my dear Lanyon and save

"Your friend,

"H.J.

"P.S.—I had already sealed this up when a fresh terror struck upon my soul. It is possible that the post-office may fail me, and this letter not come into your hands until to-morrow morning. In that case, dear Lanyon, do my errand when it shall be most convenient for you in the course of the day;

and once more expect my messenger at midnight. It may then already be too late; and if that night passes without event, you will know that you have seen the last of Henry Jekyll."

Upon the reading of this letter, I made sure my colleague was insane; but till that was proved beyond the possibility of doubt, I felt bound to do as he requested. The less I understood of this farrago, the less I was in a position to judge of its importance; and an appeal so worded could not be set aside without a grave responsibility. I rose accordingly from table, got into a hansom, and drove straight to Jekyll's house. The butler was awaiting my arrival; he had received by the same post as mine a registered letter of instruction, and had sent at once for a locksmith and a carpenter. The tradesmen came while we were yet speaking; and we moved in a body to old Dr. Denman's surgical theatre, from which (as you are doubtless aware) Jekyll's private cabinet is most conveniently entered. The door was very strong, the lock excellent; the carpenter avowed he would have great trouble and have to do much damage, if force were to be used; and the locksmith was near despair. But this last was a handy fellow, and after two hour's work, the door stood open. The press marked E was unlocked; and I took out the drawer, had it filled up with straw and tied in a sheet, and returned with it to Cavendish Square.

Here I proceeded to examine its contents. The powders were neatly enough made up, but not with the nicety of the dispensing chemist; so that it was plain they were of Jekyll's private manufacture; and when I opened one of the wrappers I found what seemed to me a simple crystalline salt of a white colour. The phial, to which I next turned my attention, might have been about half full of a blood-red liquor, which was highly pungent to the sense of smell and seemed to me to contain phosphorus and some volatile ether. At the other ingredients I could make no guess. The book was an ordinary version book and contained little but a series of dates. These covered a period of many years, but I observed that the entries ceased nearly a year ago and quite abruptly. Here and there a brief remark was appended to a date, usually no more than a single word: "double" occurring perhaps six times in a total of several hundred entries; and once very early in the list and followed by several marks of exclamation, "total failure!!!" All this, though it whetted my curiosity, told me little that was definite. Here were a phial of some salt, and the record of a series of experiments that had led (like too many of Jekyll's investigations) to no end of practical usefulness. How could the presence of these articles in my house affect either the honour, the sanity, or the life of my flighty colleague? If his messenger could go to one place, why could he not go to another? And even granting some impediment, why was this

gentleman to be received by me in secret? The more I reflected the more convinced I grew that I was dealing with a case of
cerebral disease; and though I dismissed my servants to bed, I
loaded an old revolver that I might be found in some posture
of self-defence.

Twelve o'clock had scarce rung out over London, ere the
knocker sounded very gently on the door. I went myself at the
summons, and found a small man crouching against the pil-
lars of the portico.

"Are you come from Dr. Jekyll?" I asked.

He told me "yes" by a constrained gesture; and when I had
bidden him enter, he did not obey me without a searching
backward glance into the darkness of the square. There was a
policeman not far off, advancing with his bull's eye open; and
at the sight, I thought my visitor started and made greater
haste.

These particulars struck me, I confess, disagreeably; and as
I followed him into the bright light of the consulting room,
I kept my hand ready on my weapon. Here, at last, I had a
chance of clearly seeing him. I had never set eyes on him
before, so much was certain. He was small, as I have said; I

was struck besides with the shocking expression of his face, with his remarkable combination of great muscular activity and great apparent debility of constitution, and—last but not least—with the odd, subjective disturbance caused by his neighbourhood. This bore some resemblance to incipient rigour, and was accompanied by a marked sinking of the pulse. At the time, I set it down to some idiosyncratic, personal distaste, and merely wondered at the acuteness of the symptoms; but I have since had reason to believe the cause to lie much deeper in the nature of man, and to turn on some nobler hinge than the principle of hatred.

This person (who had thus, from the first moment of his entrance, struck in me what I can only describe as a disgustful curiosity) was dressed in a fashion that would have made an ordinary person laughable; his clothes, that is to say, although they were of rich and sober fabric, were enormously too large for him in every measurement—the trousers hanging on his legs and rolled up to keep them from the ground, the waist of the coat below his haunches, and the collar sprawling wide upon his shoulders. Strange to relate, this ludicrous accoutrement was far from moving me to laughter. Rather, as there was something abnormal and misbegotten in the very essence of the creature that now faced me—something seizing, surprising and revolting—this fresh disparity seemed but to fit in with and to reinforce it; so that to my interest in the man's nature and character, there was added a curiosity as to his origin, his life, his fortune and status in the world.

These observations, though they have taken so great a space to be set down in, were yet the work of a few seconds. My visitor was, indeed, on fire with sombre excitement.

"Have you got it?" he cried. "Have you got it?" And so lively was his impatience that he even laid his hand upon my arm and sought to shake me.

I put him back, conscious at his touch of a certain icy pang along my blood. "Come, sir," said I. "You forget that I have not yet the pleasure of your acquaintance. Be seated, if you please." And I showed him an example, and sat down myself in my customary seat and with as fair an imitation of my ordinary manner to a patient, as the lateness of the hour, the nature of my preoccupations, and the horror I had of my visitor, would suffer me to muster.

"I beg your pardon, Dr. Lanyon," he replied civilly enough. "What you say is very well founded; and my impatience has shown its heels to my politeness. I come here at the instance of your colleague, Dr. Henry Jekyll, on a piece of business of some moment; and I understood..." He paused and put his hand to his throat, and I could see, in spite of his collected manner, that he was wrestling against the approaches of the hysteria—"I understood, a drawer..."

But here I took pity on my visitor's suspense, and some perhaps on my own growing curiosity.

"There it is, sir," said I, pointing to the drawer, where it lay on the floor behind a table and still covered with the sheet.

He sprang to it, and then paused, and laid his hand upon his heart; I could hear his teeth grate with the convulsive action of his jaws; and his face was so ghastly to see that I grew alarmed both for his life and reason.

"Compose yourself," said I.

He turned a dreadful smile to me, and as if with the decision of despair, plucked away the sheet. At sight of the contents, he uttered one loud sob of such immense relief that I sat petrified. And the next moment, in a voice that was already fairly well under control, "Have you a graduated glass?" he asked.

I rose from my place with something of an effort and gave him what he asked.

He thanked me with a smiling nod, measured out a few minims of the red tincture and added one of the powders. The mixture, which was at first of a reddish hue, began, in proportion as the crystals melted, to brighten in colour, to effervesce audibly, and to throw off small fumes of vapour. Suddenly and at the same moment, the ebullition ceased and the compound changed to a dark purple, which faded again more slowly to a watery green. My visitor, who had watched these metamorphoses with a keen eye, smiled, set down the glass upon the table, and then turned and looked upon me with an air of scrutiny.

"And now," said he, "to settle what remains. Will you be wise? will you be guided? will you suffer me to take this glass in my hand and to go forth from your house without further parley? or has the greed of curiosity too much command of you? Think before you answer, for it shall be done as you decide. As you decide, you shall be left as you were before, and neither richer nor wiser, unless the sense of service rendered to a man in mortal distress may be counted as a kind of riches of the soul. Or, if you shall so prefer to choose, a new province of knowledge and new avenues to fame and power shall be laid open to you, here, in this room, upon the instant; and your sight shall be blasted by a prodigy to stagger the unbelief of Satan."

"Sir," said I, affecting a coolness that I was far from truly possessing, "you speak enigmas, and you will perhaps not wonder that I hear you with no very strong impression of belief. But I have gone too far in the way of inexplicable services to pause before I see the end."

"It is well," replied my visitor. "Lanyon, you remember your vows: what follows is under the seal of our profession. And now, you who have so long been bound to the most narrow and material views, you who have denied the virtue of transcendental medicine, you who have derided your superiors— behold!"

He put the glass to his lips and drank at one gulp. A cry followed; he reeled, staggered, clutched at the table and held on, staring with injected eyes, gasping with open mouth; and as I looked there came, I thought, a change—he seemed to swell— his face became suddenly black and the features seemed to melt and alter—and the next moment, I had sprung to my feet and leaped back against the wall, my arms raised to shield me from that prodigy, my mind submerged in terror.

"O God!" I screamed, and "O God!" again and again; for there before my eyes—pale and shaken, and half fainting, and groping before him with his hands, like a man restored from death—there stood Henry Jekyll!

What he told me in the next hour, I cannot bring my mind to set on paper. I saw what I saw, I heard what I heard, and my soul sickened at it; and yet now when that sight has faded from my eyes, I ask myself if I believe it, and I cannot answer. My life is shaken to its roots; sleep has left me; the deadliest terror sits by me at all hours of the day and night; and I feel that my days are numbered, and that I must die; and yet I shall die incredulous. As for the moral turpitude that man unveiled to me, even with tears of penitence, I cannot, even in memory, dwell on it without a start of horror. I will say but one thing, Utterson, and that (if you can bring your mind to credit it) will be more than enough. The creature who crept into my house that night was, on Jekyll's own confession, known by the name of Hyde and hunted for in every corner of the land as the murderer of Carew.

HASTIE LANYON.

Chapter

Henry Jekyll's Full Statement of the Case

10

All human beings, as we meet them,
are commingled out of good and evil:
and Edward Hyde, alone in the ranks of mankind, was pure evil.

I was born in the year 18— to a large fortune, endowed besides with excellent parts, inclined by nature to industry, fond
of the respect of the wise and good among my fellowmen, and
thus, as might have been supposed, with every guarantee of
an honourable and distinguished future. And indeed the worst
of my faults was a certain impatient gaiety of disposition, such
as has made the happiness of many, but such as I found it
hard to reconcile with my imperious desire to carry my head
high, and wear a more than commonly grave countenance before the public. Hence it came about that I concealed my pleasures; and that when I reached years of reflection, and began
to look round me and take stock of my progress and position
in the world, I stood already committed to a profound duplic-
ity of life. Many a man would have even blazoned such irreg-
ularities as I was guilty of; but from the high views that I had
set before me, I regarded and hid them with an almost morbid
sense of shame. It was thus rather the exacting nature of my
aspirations than any particular degradation in my faults, that
made me what I was, and, with even a deeper trench than in
the majority of men, severed in me those provinces of good
and ill which divide and compound man's dual nature. In this
case, I was driven to reflect deeply and inveterately on that
hard law of life, which lies at the root of religion and is one
of the most plentiful springs of distress. Though so profound
a double-dealer, I was in no sense a hypocrite; both sides of

me were in dead earnest; I was no more myself when I laid aside restraint and plunged in shame, than when I laboured, in the eye of day, at the furtherance of knowledge or the relief of sorrow and suffering. And it chanced that the direction of my scientific studies, which led wholly towards the mystic and the transcendental, reacted and shed a strong light on this consciousness of the perennial war among my members. With every day, and from both sides of my intelligence, the moral and the intellectual, I thus drew steadily nearer to that truth, by whose partial discovery I have been doomed to such a dreadful shipwreck: that man is not truly one, but truly two. I say two, because the state of my own knowledge does not pass beyond that point. Others will follow, others will outstrip me on the same lines; and I hazard the guess that man will be ultimately known for a mere polity of multifarious, incongruous and independent denizens. I, for my part, from the nature of my life, advanced infallibly in one direction and in one direction only. It was on the moral side, and in my own person, that I learned to recognise the thorough and primitive duality of man; I saw that, of the two natures that contended in the field of my consciousness, even if I could rightly be said to be either, it was only because I was radically both; and from an early date, even before the course of my scientific discoveries had begun to suggest the most naked possibility of such a miracle, I had learned to dwell with pleasure, as a beloved daydream, on the thought of the separation of these elements. If each, I told myself, could be housed in separate identities, life would be relieved of all that was unbearable; the unjust might go his way, delivered from the aspirations and remorse of his more upright twin; and the just could walk steadfastly and securely on his upward path, doing the good things in which he found his pleasure, and no longer exposed to disgrace and penitence by the hands of this extraneous evil. It was the curse of mankind that these incongruous faggots were thus bound together—that in the agonised womb of consciousness, these polar twins should be continuously struggling. How, then were they dissociated?

I was so far in my reflections when, as I have said, a side light began to shine upon the subject from the laboratory table. I began to perceive more deeply than it has ever yet been stated, the trembling immateriality, the mistlike transience, of this seemingly so solid body in which we walk attired. Certain agents I found to have the power to shake and pluck back that fleshly vestment, even as a wind might toss the curtains of a pavilion. For two good reasons, I will not enter deeply into this scientific branch of my confession. First, because I have been made to learn that the doom and burthen of our life is bound for ever on man's shoulders, and when the attempt is made to cast it off, it but returns upon us with more unfamiliar and more awful pressure. Second, because, as my narrative will make, alas! too evident, my discoveries were incomplete. Enough then, that I not only recognised my natural body from the mere aura and effulgence of certain of the powers that made up my spirit, but managed to compound a drug by which these powers should be dethroned from their supremacy, and a second form and countenance substituted, none the less natural to me because they were the expression, and bore the stamp of lower elements in my soul.

I hesitated long before I put this theory to the test of practice. I knew well that I risked death; for any drug that so potently controlled and shook the very fortress of identity, might, by the least scruple of an overdose or at the least inopportunity in the moment of exhibition, utterly blot out that immaterial tabernacle which I looked to it to change. But the temptation of a discovery so singular and profound at last overcame the suggestions of alarm. I had long since prepared my tincture; I purchased at once, from a firm of wholesale chemists, a large quantity of a particular salt which I knew, from my experiments, to be the last ingredient required; and late one accursed night, I compounded the elements, watched them boil and smoke together in the glass, and when the ebullition had subsided, with a strong glow of courage, drank off the potion.

The most racking pangs succeeded: a grinding in the bones, deadly nausea, and a horror of the spirit that cannot be exceeded at the hour of birth or death. Then these agonies began swiftly to subside, and I came to myself as if out of a great sickness. There was something strange in my sensations, something indescribably new and, from its very novelty, incredibly sweet. I felt younger, lighter, happier in body; within I was conscious of a heady recklessness, a current of disordered sensual images running like a millrace in my fancy, a solution of the bonds of obligation, an unknown but not an innocent freedom of the soul. I knew myself, at the first breath of this new life, to be more wicked, tenfold more wicked, sold a slave to my original evil; and the thought, in that moment, braced and delighted me like wine. I stretched out my hands, exulting in the freshness of these sensations; and in the act, I was suddenly aware that I had lost in stature.

There was no mirror, at that date, in my room; that which stands beside me as I write, was brought there later on and for the very purpose of these transformations. The night, however, was far gone into the morning—the morning, black as it was, was nearly ripe for the conception of the day—the inmates of my house were locked in the most rigorous hours of slumber; and I determined, flushed as I was with hope and triumph, to venture in my new shape as far as to my bedroom.

I crossed the yard, wherein the constellations looked down upon me, I could have thought, with wonder, the first creature of that sort that their unsleeping vigilance had yet disclosed to them; I stole through the corridors, a stranger in my own house; and coming to my room, I saw for the first time the appearance of Edward Hyde.

I must here speak by theory alone, saying not that which I know, but that which I suppose to be most probable. The evil side of my nature, to which I had now transferred the stamping efficacy, was less robust and less developed than the good which I had just deposed. Again, in the course of my life, which had been, after all, nine tenths a life of effort, virtue and control, it had been much less exercised and much less exhausted. And hence, as I think, it came about that Edward Hyde was so much smaller, slighter and younger than Henry Jekyll. Even as good shone upon the countenance of the one, evil was written broadly and plainly on the face of the other. Evil besides (which I must still believe to be the lethal side of man) had left on that body an imprint of deformity and decay. And yet when I looked upon that ugly idol in the glass, I was conscious of no repugnance, rather of a leap of welcome. This, too, was myself. It seemed natural and human. In my eyes it bore a livelier image of the spirit, it seemed more express and single, than the imperfect and divided countenance I had been hitherto accustomed to call mine. And in so far I was doubtless right. I have observed that when I wore the semblance of Edward Hyde, none could come near to me at first without a visible misgiving of the flesh. This, as I take it, was because all human beings, as we meet them, are commingled out of good and evil: and Edward Hyde, alone in the ranks of mankind, was pure evil.

I lingered but a moment at the mirror: the second and conclusive experiment had yet to be attempted; it yet remained to be seen if I had lost my identity beyond redemption and must flee before daylight from a house that was no longer mine; and hurrying back to my cabinet, I once more prepared and drank the cup, once more suffered the pangs of dissolution, and came to myself once more with the character, the stature and the face of Henry Jekyll.

That night I had come to the fatal cross-roads. Had I approached my discovery in a more noble spirit, had I risked the experiment while under the empire of generous or pious aspirations, all must have been otherwise, and from these agonies of death and birth, I had come forth an angel instead of a fiend. The drug had no discriminating action; it was neither diabolical nor divine; it but shook the doors of the prison-house of my disposition; and like the captives of Philippi, that

which stood within ran forth. At that time my virtue slumbered; my evil, kept awake by ambition, was alert and swift
to seize the occasion; and the thing that was projected was
Edward Hyde. Hence, although I had now two characters as
well as two appearances, one was wholly evil, and the other
was still the old Henry Jekyll, that incongruous compound of
whose reformation and improvement I had already learned to
despair. The movement was thus wholly toward the worse.

Even at that time, I had not yet conquered my aversions to
the dryness of a life of study. I would still be merrily disposed
at times; and as my pleasures were (to say the least) undignified, and I was not only well known and highly considered,
but growing towards the elderly man, this incoherency of my
life was daily growing more unwelcome. It was on this side
that my new power tempted me until I fell in slavery. I had
but to drink the cup, to doff at once the body of the noted
professor, and to assume, like a thick cloak, that of Edward
Hyde. I smiled at the notion; it seemed to me at the time to be
humourous; and I made my preparations with the most stu-
dious care. I took and furnished that house in Soho, to which
Hyde was tracked by the police; and engaged as a housekeep-
er a creature whom I knew well to be silent and unscrupu-
lous. On the other side, I announced to my servants that a Mr.
Hyde (whom I described) was to have full liberty and power

217

about my house in the square; and to parry mishaps, I even called and made myself a familiar object, in my second character. I next drew up that will to which you so much objected; so that if anything befell me in the person of Dr. Jekyll, I could enter on that of Edward Hyde without pecuniary loss. And thus fortified, as I supposed, on every side, I began to profit by the strange immunities of my position.

Men have before hired bravos to transact their crimes, while their own person and reputation sat under shelter. I was the first that ever did so for his pleasures. I was the first that could plod in the public eye with a load of genial respectability, and in a moment, like a schoolboy, strip off these lendings and spring headlong into the sea of liberty. But for me, in my impenetrable mantle, the safety was complete. Think of it—I did not even exist! Let me but escape into my laboratory door, give me but a second or two to mix and swallow the draught that I had always standing ready; and whatever he had done, Edward Hyde would pass away like the stain of breath upon a mirror; and there in his stead, quietly at home, trimming the midnight lamp in his study, a man who could afford to laugh at suspicion, would be Henry Jekyll.

The pleasures which I made haste to seek in my disguise were, as I have said, undignified; I would scarce use a harder term. But in the hands of Edward Hyde, they soon began to turn toward the monstrous. When I would come back from these excursions, I was often plunged into a kind of wonder at my vicarious depravity. This familiar that I called out of my own soul, and sent forth alone to do his good pleasure, was a being inherently malign and villainous; his every act and thought centered on self; drinking pleasure with bestial avidity from any degree of torture to another; relentless like a man of stone. Henry Jekyll stood at times aghast before the acts of Edward Hyde; but the situation was apart from ordinary laws, and insidiously relaxed the grasp of conscience. It was Hyde, after all, and Hyde alone, that was guilty. Jekyll was no worse; he woke again to his good qualities seemingly unimpaired; he would even make haste, where it was possible, to undo the evil done by Hyde. And thus his conscience slumbered.

Into the details of the infamy at which I thus connived (for even now I can scarce grant that I committed it) I have no design of entering; I mean but to point out the warnings and the successive steps with which my chastisement approached. I met with one accident which, as it brought on no consequence, I shall no more than mention. An act of cruelty to a child aroused against me the anger of a passer-by, whom I recognised the other day in the person of your kinsman; the doctor and the child's family joined him; there were moments when I feared for my life; and at last, in order to pacify their too just resentment, Edward Hyde had to bring them to the door, and pay them in a cheque drawn in the name of Henry Jekyll. But this danger was easily eliminated from the future, by opening an account at another bank in the name of Edward Hyde himself; and when, by sloping my own hand backward, I had supplied my double with a signature, I thought I sat beyond the reach of fate.

Some two months before the murder of Sir Danvers, I had been out for one of my adventures, had returned at a late hour, and woke the next day in bed with somewhat odd sensations. It was in vain I looked about me; in vain I saw the decent furniture and tall proportions of my room in the square; in vain that I recognised the pattern of the bed curtains and the design of the mahogany frame; something still kept insisting that I was not where I was, that I had not wakened where I seemed to be, but in the little room in Soho where I was accustomed to sleep in the body of Edward Hyde. I smiled to myself, and in my psychological way, began lazily to inquire into the elements of this illusion, occasionally, even as I did so, dropping back into a comfortable morning doze. I was still so engaged when, in one of my more wakeful moments, my eyes fell upon my hand. Now the hand of Henry Jekyll (as you have often remarked) was professional in shape and size;

it was large, firm, white and comely. But the hand which I now saw, clearly enough, in the yellow light of a mid-London morning, lying half shut on the bedclothes, was lean, corded, knuckly, of a dusky pallor and thickly shaded with a swart growth of hair. It was the hand of Edward Hyde.

I must have stared upon it for near half a minute, sunk as I was in the mere stupidity of wonder, before terror woke up in my breast as sudden and startling as the crash of cymbals; and bounding from my bed I rushed to the mirror. At the sight that met my eyes, my blood was changed into something exquisitely thin and icy. Yes, I had gone to bed Henry Jekyll, I had awakened Edward Hyde. How was this to be explained? I asked myself; and then, with another bound of terror—how was it to be remedied? It was well on in the morning; the servants were up; all my drugs were in the cabinet—a long journey down two pairs of stairs, through the back passage, across the open court and through the anatomical theatre, from where I was then standing horror-struck. It might indeed be possible to cover my face; but of what use was that, when I was unable to conceal the alteration in my stature? And then with an overpowering sweetness of relief, it came back upon my mind that the servants were already used to the coming and going of my second self. I had soon dressed, as well as I was able, in clothes of my own size: had soon passed through the house, where Bradshaw stared and drew back at seeing Mr. Hyde at such an hour and in such a strange array; and ten minutes later, Dr. Jekyll had returned to his own shape and was sitting down, with a darkened brow, to make a feint of breakfasting.

Small indeed was my appetite. This inexplicable incident, this reversal of my previous experience, seemed, like the Babylonian finger on the wall, to be spelling out the letters of my judgment; and I began to reflect more seriously than ever before on the issues and possibilities of my double existence. That part of me which I had the power of projecting, had lately been much exercised and nourished; it had seemed to me of late as though the body of Edward Hyde had grown in stature, as though (when I wore that form) I were conscious of a more generous tide of blood; and I began to spy a danger that, if this were much prolonged, the balance of my nature might be permanently overthrown, the power of voluntary change be forfeited, and the character of Edward Hyde become irrevocably mine. The power of the drug had not been always equally displayed. Once, very early in my career, it had totally failed me; since then I had been obliged on more than one occasion to double, and once, with infinite risk of death, to treble the amount; and these rare uncertainties had cast hitherto the sole shadow on my contentment. Now, however, and in the light of that morning's accident, I was led to remark that whereas, in the beginning, the difficulty had been to throw off the body of Jekyll, it had of late gradually but decidedly transferred itself to the other side. All things therefore seemed to point to this; that I was slowly losing hold of my original and better self, and becoming slowly incorporated with my second and worse.

Between these two, I now felt I had to choose. My two natures had memory in common, but all other faculties were most unequally shared between them. Jekyll (who was composite) now with the most sensitive apprehensions, now with a greedy gusto, projected and shared in the pleasures and adventures of Hyde; but Hyde was indifferent to Jekyll, or but remembered him as the mountain bandit remembers the cavern in which he conceals himself from pursuit. Jekyll had more than a father's interest; Hyde had more than a son's indifference. To cast in my lot with Jekyll, was to die to those appetites which I had long secretly indulged and had of late begun to pamper. To cast it in with Hyde, was to die to a thousand interests and aspirations, and to become, at a blow and forever, despised and friendless. The bargain might appear unequal; but there was still another consideration in the scales; for while Jekyll would suffer smartingly in the fires of abstinence, Hyde would be not even conscious of all that he had lost. Strange as my circumstances were, the terms of this debate are as old and commonplace as man; much the same inducements and alarms cast the die for any tempted and trembling sinner; and it fell out with me, as it falls with so vast a majority of my fellows, that I chose the better part and was found wanting in the strength to keep to it.

Yes, I preferred the elderly and discontented doctor, surrounded by friends and cherishing honest hopes; and bade a resolute farewell to the liberty, the comparative youth, the light step, leaping impulses and secret pleasures, that I had enjoyed in the disguise of Hyde. I made this choice perhaps with some unconscious reservation, for I neither gave up the house in Soho, nor destroyed the clothes of Edward Hyde, which still lay ready in my cabinet. For two months, however, I was true to my determination; for two months, I led a life of such severity as I had never before attained to, and enjoyed the compensations of an approving conscience. But time began at last to obliterate the freshness of my alarm; the praises of conscience began to grow into a thing of course; I began to be tortured with throes and longings, as of Hyde struggling after freedom; and at last, in an hour of moral weakness, I once again compounded and swallowed the transforming draught.

I do not suppose that, when a drunkard reasons with himself upon his vice, he is once out of five hundred times affected by the dangers that he runs through his brutish, physical insensibility; neither had I, long as I had considered my position, made enough allowance for the complete moral insensibility and insensate readiness to evil, which were the leading characters of Edward Hyde. Yet it was by these that I was punished. My devil had been long caged, he came out roaring. I was conscious, even when I took the draught, of a more unbridled, a more furious propensity to ill. It must have been this, I suppose, that stirred in my soul that tempest of impatience with which I listened to the civilities of my unhappy victim; I declare, at least, before God, no man morally sane could have been guilty of that crime upon so pitiful a provocation; and that I struck in no more reasonable spirit than that in which a sick child may break a plaything. But I had voluntarily stripped myself of all those balancing instincts by which even the worst of us continues to walk with some degree of steadiness among temptations; and in my case, to be tempted, however slightly, was to fall.

Instantly the spirit of hell awoke in me and raged. With a transport of glee, I mauled the unresisting body, tasting delight from every blow; and it was not till weariness had begun to succeed, that I was suddenly, in the top fit of my delirium, struck through the heart by a cold thrill of terror. A mist dispersed; I saw my life to be forfeit; and fled from the scene of these excesses, at once glorying and trembling, my lust of evil gratified and stimulated, my love of life screwed to the topmost peg. I ran to the house in Soho, and (to make assurance doubly sure) destroyed my papers; thence I set out through the lamplit streets, in the same divided ecstasy of mind, gloating on my crime, light-headedly devising others in the future, and yet still hastening and still hearkening in my wake for the steps of the avenger. Hyde had a song upon his lips as he compounded the draught, and as he drank it, pledged the dead man. The pangs of transformation had not done tearing him, before Henry Jekyll, with streaming tears of gratitude and remorse, had fallen upon his knees and lifted his clasped hands to God. The veil of self-indulgence was rent from head to foot. I saw my life as a whole: I followed it up from the days of childhood, when I had walked with my father's hand, and through the self-denying toils of my professional life, to arrive again and again, with the same sense of unreality, at the damned horrors of the evening. I could have screamed aloud; I sought with tears and prayers to smother down the crowd of hideous images and sounds with which my memory swarmed against me; and still, between the petitions, the ugly face of my iniquity stared into my soul. As the acuteness of this remorse began to die away, it was succeeded by a sense of joy.

The problem of my conduct was solved. Hyde was thenceforth impossible; whether I would or not, I was now confined to the better part of my existence; and O, how I rejoiced to think of it! with what willing humility I embraced anew the restrictions of natural life! with what sincere renunciation I locked the door by which I had so often gone and come, and ground the key under my heel!

The next day, came the news that the murder had been overlooked, that the guilt of Hyde was patent to the world, and that the victim was a man high in public estimation. It was not only a crime, it had been a tragic folly. I think I was glad to know it; I think I was glad to have my better impulses thus buttressed and guarded by the terrors of the scaffold. Jekyll was now my city of refuge; let but Hyde peep out an instant, and the hands of all men would be raised to take and slay him.

I resolved in my future conduct to redeem the past; and I can say with honesty that my resolve was fruitful of some good. You know yourself how earnestly, in the last months of the last year, I laboured to relieve suffering; you know that much was done for others, and that the days passed quietly, almost happily for myself. Nor can I truly say that I wearied of this beneficent and innocent life; I think instead that I daily enjoyed it more completely; but I was still cursed with my duality of purpose; and as the first edge of my penitence wore off, the lower side of me, so long indulged, so recently chained down, began to growl for licence. Not that I dreamed of resuscitating Hyde; the bare idea of that would startle me to frenzy: no, it was in my own person that I was once more tempted to trifle with my conscience; and it was as an ordinary secret sinner that I at last fell before the assaults of temptation.

There comes an end to all things; the most capacious measure is filled at last; and this brief condescension to my evil finally destroyed the balance of my soul. And yet I was not alarmed; the fall seemed natural, like a return to the old days before I had made my discovery. It was a fine, clear, January day, wet under foot where the frost had melted, but cloudless overhead; and the Regent's Park was full of winter chirrupings and sweet with spring odours. I sat in the sun on a bench; the animal within me licking the chops of memory; the spiritual side a little drowsed, promising subsequent penitence, but not yet moved to begin. After all, I reflected, I was like my neighbours; and then I smiled, comparing myself with other men, comparing my active good-will with the lazy cruelty of their neglect. And at the very moment of that vainglorious thought, a qualm came over me, a horrid nausea and the most deadly shuddering. These passed away, and left me faint; and then as in its turn faintness subsided, I began to be aware of a change in the temper of my thoughts, a greater boldness, a contempt of danger, a solution of the bonds of obligation. I looked down; my clothes hung formlessly on my shrunken limbs; the hand that lay on my knee was corded and hairy. I was once more Edward Hyde. A moment before I had been safe of all men's respect, wealthy, beloved—the cloth laying for me in the dining-room at home; and now I was the common quarry of mankind, hunted, houseless, a known murderer, thrall to the gallows.

My reason wavered, but it did not fail me utterly. I have more than once observed that in my second character, my faculties seemed sharpened to a point and my spirits more tensely elastic; thus it came about that, where Jekyll perhaps might have succumbed, Hyde rose to the importance of the moment. My drugs were in one of the presses of my cabinet; how was I to reach them? That was the problem that (crushing my temples in my hands) I set myself to solve. The laboratory door I had closed. If I sought to enter by the house, my own servants would consign me to the gallows. I saw I must employ another hand, and thought of Lanyon. How was he to be reached? how persuaded? Supposing that I escaped capture in the streets, how was I to make my way into his presence?

and how should I, an unknown and displeasing visitor, prevail on the famous physician to rifle the study of his colleague, Dr. Jekyll? Then I remembered that of my original character, one part remained to me: I could write my own hand; and once I had conceived that kindling spark, the way that I must follow became lighted up from end to end.

Thereupon, I arranged my clothes as best I could, and summoning a passing hansom, drove to an hotel in Portland Street, the name of which I chanced to remember. At my appearance (which was indeed comical enough, however tragic a fate these garments covered) the driver could not conceal his mirth. I gnashed my teeth upon him with a gust of devilish fury; and the smile withered from his face—happily for him—yet more happily for myself, for in another instant I had certainly dragged him from his perch. At the inn, as I entered, I looked about me with so black a countenance as made the attendants tremble; not a look did they exchange in my presence; but obsequiously took my orders, led me to a private room, and brought me wherewithal to write. Hyde in danger of his life was a creature new to me; shaken with inordinate anger, strung to the pitch of murder, lusting to inflict pain. Yet the creature was astute; mastered his fury with a great effort of the will; composed his two important letters, one to Lanyon and one to Poole; and that he might receive actual evidence of their being posted, sent them out with directions that they should be registered. Thenceforward, he sat all day over the fire in the private room, gnawing his nails; there he dined, sitting alone with his fears, the waiter visibly quailing before his eye; and thence, when the night was fully come, he set forth in the corner of a closed cab, and was driven to and fro about the streets of the city. He, I say—I cannot say, I. That child of Hell had nothing human; nothing lived in him but fear and hatred. And when at last, thinking the driver had begun to grow suspicious, he discharged the cab and ventured on foot, attired in his misfitting clothes, an object marked out for observation, into the midst of the nocturnal passengers, these two base passions raged within him like a tempest. He walked fast, hunted by his fears, chattering to himself, skulking through the less frequented thoroughfares, counting the minutes that still divided him from midnight. Once a woman spoke to him, offering, I think, a box of lights. He smote her in the face, and she fled.

When I came to myself at Lanyon's, the horror of my old friend perhaps affected me somewhat: I do not know; it was at least but a drop in the sea to the abhorrence with which I looked back upon these hours. A change had come over me. It was no longer the fear of the gallows, it was the horror of being Hyde that racked me. I received Lanyon's condemnation partly in a dream; it was partly in a dream that I came home to my own house and got into bed. I slept after the prostration of the day, with a stringent and profound slumber which not even the nightmares that wrung me could avail to break. I awoke in the morning shaken, weakened, but refreshed. I still hated and feared the thought of the brute that slept within me, and I had not of course forgotten the appalling dangers of the day before; but I was once more at home, in my own house and close to my drugs; and gratitude for my escape shone so strong in my soul that it almost rivalled the brightness of hope.

I was stepping leisurely across the court after breakfast, drinking the chill of the air with pleasure, when I was seized again with those indescribable sensations that heralded the change; and I had but the time to gain the shelter of my cabinet, before I was once again raging and freezing with the passions of Hyde. It took on this occasion a double dose to recall me to myself; and alas! six hours after, as I sat looking sadly in the fire, the pangs returned, and the drug had to be re-administered. In short, from that day forth it seemed only by a great effort as of gymnastics, and only under the immediate stimulation of the drug, that I was able to wear the countenance of Jekyll. At all hours of the day and night, I would be taken with the premonitory shudder; above all, if I slept, or even dozed for a moment in my chair, it was always as Hyde that I awakened. Under the strain of this continually impending doom and by the sleeplessness to which I now condemned myself, ay, even beyond what I had thought possible to man, I became, in my own person, a creature eaten up and emptied by fever, languidly weak both in body and mind, and solely occupied by one thought: the horror of my other self. But when I slept, or when the virtue of the medicine wore off, I would leap almost without transition (for the pangs of transformation grew daily less marked) into the possession of a fancy brimming with images of terror, a soul boiling with causeless hatreds, and a body that seemed not strong enough to contain the raging energies of life. The powers of Hyde seemed to have grown with the sickliness of Jekyll. And certainly the hate that now divided them was equal on each side. With Jekyll, it was a thing of vital instinct. He had now seen the full deformity of that creature that shared with him some of the phenomena of consciousness, and was co-heir with him to death: and beyond these links of community, which in themselves made the most poignant part of his distress, he thought of Hyde, for all his energy of life, as of something not only hellish but inorganic. This was the shocking thing; that the slime of the pit seemed to utter cries and voices; that the amorphous dust gesticulated and sinned; that what was dead, and had no shape, should usurp the offices of life. And this again, that that insurgent horror was knit to him closer than a wife, closer than an eye; lay caged in his flesh, where he heard it mutter and felt it struggle to be born; and at every hour of weakness, and in the confidence of slumber, prevailed against him, and deposed him out of life. The hatred of Hyde for Jekyll was of a different order. His terror of the gallows drove him continually to commit temporary suicide, and return to his subordinate station of a part instead of a person; but he loathed the necessity, he loathed the despondency into which Jekyll was now fallen, and he resented the dislike with which he was himself regarded. Hence the ape-like tricks that he would play me, scrawling in my own hand blasphemies on the pages of my books, burning the letters and destroying the portrait of my father; and indeed, had it not been for his fear of death, he would long ago have ruined himself in order to involve me in the ruin. But his love of life is wonderful; I go further: I, who sicken and freeze at the mere thought of him, when I recall the abjection and passion of this attachment, and when I know how he fears my power to cut him off by suicide, I find it in my heart to pity him.

It is useless, and the time awfully fails me, to prolong this description; no one has ever suffered such torments, let that suffice; and yet even to these, habit brought—no, not allevia-tion—but a certain callousness of soul, a certain acquiescence of despair; and my punishment might have gone on for years, but for the last calamity which has now fallen, and which has finally severed me from my own face and nature. My provision of the salt, which had never been renewed since the date of the first experiment, began to run low. I sent out for a fresh supply and mixed the draught; the ebullition followed, and the first change of colour, not the second; I drank it and it was without efficiency. You will learn from Poole how I have had London ransacked; it was in vain; and I am now persuaded that my first supply was impure, and that it was that unknown impurity which lent efficacy to the draught.

About a week has passed, and I am now finishing this statement under the influence of the last of the old powders. This, then, is the last time, short of a miracle, that Henry Jekyll can think his own thoughts or see his own face (now how sadly altered!) in the glass. Nor must I delay too long to bring my writing to an end; for if my narrative has hitherto escaped destruction, it has been by a combination of great prudence and great good luck. Should the throes of change take me in the act of writing it, Hyde will tear it in pieces; but if some time shall have elapsed after I have laid it by, his wonderful selfishness and circumscription to the moment will probably save it once again from the action of his ape-like spite. And indeed the doom that is closing on us both has already changed and crushed him. Half an hour from now, when I shall again and forever reindue that hated personality, I know how I shall sit shuddering and weeping in my chair, or continue, with the most strained and fearstruck ecstasy of listening, to pace up and down this room (my last earthly refuge) and give ear to every sound of menace. Will Hyde die upon the scaffold? or will he find courage to release himself at the last moment? God knows; I am careless; this is my true hour of death, and what is to follow concerns another than myself. Here then, as I lay down the pen and proceed to seal up my confession, I bring the life of that unhappy Henry Jekyll to an end.

Robert Louis Stevenson

羅伯特·路易斯·史蒂文森 生平年表

年份	歲數	事件
1850	0	羅伯特·路易斯·史蒂文森（Robert Louis Stevenson）生於蘇格蘭首都愛丁堡，父親、祖父、曾祖父都是著名的燈塔設計師與工程師。自幼體弱多病的他有著熱愛冒險、喜愛海洋的性格。
1861	11	史蒂文森的身體已經好轉了，父母送他到愛丁堡學校就讀，準備將來進入愛丁堡大學，他們計畫讓史蒂文森成為燈塔工程師。在這段時期，史蒂文森廣泛的閱讀文學書籍，他特別喜歡莎士比亞、沃爾特·司各特、約翰·本仁與《一千零一夜》。
1867	17	進入愛丁堡大學就讀後，很快地就發現他對於科學或物理並沒有天份，無法成為工程師。在他與父親經歷一次旅行之後，史蒂文森發現比起建造燈塔，他對這些關於他們所遊歷的島嶼及海岸的奇妙傳奇故事更為著迷。
1868	18	在 18 歲時，將原本的名字 Robert Lewis Balfour Stevenson 中間名去掉，並把 Lewis 改為 Louis，自此簡稱為 RLS。
1875	25	在 25 歲時通過律師界的考試卻沒有開業。接下來四年時間史蒂文森在法國運河上乘坐獨木舟旅行，這段旅程中史蒂文森結交了許多朋友，並把這些經歷都寫在《內河航程》（An Inland Voyage）與《騎驢漫遊記》（Travels with a Donkey in the Cévennes）裡。
1876	26	開始在《倫敦雜誌》上連載《新天方夜譚》（New Arabian Nights），與芬妮在巴黎相遇，史蒂文森第一眼就愛上了她。
1880	30	與芬妮在舊金山結婚。

1882	32	出版《新天方夜譚》。
1883	33	出版《金銀島》（Treasure Island）是史蒂文森最著名的作品之一，一部關於海盜與寶藏的冒險小說，經常被改編電影以及電視劇。
1886	36	出版《化身博士》(Strange Case of Dr Jekyll and Mr Hyde)，一部關於多重人格的中篇小說。
1888	38	6 月時租賃了 Casco 號快艇，與家人從舊金山出發，開始了冒險之旅，海洋的空氣與冒險的刺激使得史蒂文森恢復健康。
1890	40	在航行兩年多後於薩摩亞群島的烏波盧島（Upolu）購買了 400 英畝（大約 1.6 平方公里）的土地。史蒂文森經過了許多努力，在這裡建立了自己的棲身之所，而且將它命名為維利馬（Vailima）。
1894	44	12 月 3 日早上，史蒂文森一如以往從事《赫米斯頓的韋爾》（Weir of Hermiston）的寫作，晚上史蒂文森一面與妻子談話而一面打開一瓶葡萄酒時，突然倒了下來，並在幾個鐘頭後去世，享年 44 歲，推測死因可能為中風。而他的遺作《赫米斯頓的韋爾》尚未完成。

Strange Case of Dr. Jekyll and Mr. Hyde

世界經典文學

化身博士 中英對照雙語版

2023 年 10 月 27 日　初版第一刷　定價 300 元

著　　　者	羅伯特‧路易斯‧史蒂文森
譯　　　者	陳家瑩
美術編輯	王舒玗
總 編 輯	洪季楨
編輯企劃	笛藤出版
發 行 所	八方出版股份有限公司
發 行 人	林建仲
地　　　址	台北市中山區長安東路二段 171 號 3 樓 3 室
電　　　話	(02) 2777-3682
傳　　　真	(02) 2777-3672
總 經 銷	聯合發行股份有限公司
地　　　址	新北市新店區寶橋路 235 巷 6 弄 6 號 2 樓
電　　　話	(02)2917-8022‧(02)2917-8042
製 版 廠	造極彩色印刷製版股份有限公司
地　　　址	新北市中和區中山路二段 380 巷 7 號 1 樓
電　　　話	(02)2240-0333‧(02)2248-3904
郵撥帳戶	八方出版股份有限公司
郵撥帳號	19809050

化身博士 / 羅伯特‧路易斯‧史蒂文森著 ; 陳家瑩譯 . -- 初版 .
-- 臺北市 : 笛藤出版 , 2023.10

　面 ;　公分

譯自 : Strange case of Dr Jekyll and Mr Hyde.

ISBN 978-957-710-905-7(平裝)

873.57　　　112015950